ALSO BY JAYSON GREENE

Once More We Saw Stars

UnWorld

UnWorld

JAYSON GREENE

 ALFRED A. KNOPF   NEW YORK   2025

A BORZOI BOOK
FIRST HARDCOVER EDITION
PUBLISHED BY ALFRED A. KNOPF 2025

Published by Alfred A. Knopf, a division of Penguin Random House LLC,
1745 Broadway, New York, NY 10019.

Knopf, Borzoi Books, and the colophon are registered trademarks of
Penguin Random House LLC.

LIBRARY OF CONGRESS CATALOGING-IN-PUBLICATION DATA
Names: Greene, Jayson, author.
Title: Unworld : a novel / Jayson Greene.
Description: New York : Alfred A. Knopf, 2025. | "This is a Borzoi book"—
    Title page verso. |
Identifiers: LCCN 2024034842 (print) | LCCN 2024034843 (ebook) |
    ISBN 9780593802182 (hardcover) | ISBN 9780593802199 (ebook)
Subjects: LCSH: Artificial intelligence—Fiction. | LCGFT: Science fiction. |
    Novels.
Classification: LCC PS3607.R452695 U59 2025 (print) |
    LCC PS3607.R452695 (ebook) | DDC 813/.6—dc23/eng/20241028
LC record available at https://lccn.loc.gov/2024034842
LC ebook record available at https://lccn.loc.gov/2024034843

Title page and part titles image by Anastasiia / stock.adobe.com
Back of part titles image by jackreznor / stock.adobe.com

penguinrandomhouse.com | aaknopf.com

Printed in the United States of America

The authorized representative in the EU for product safety and
compliance is Penguin Random House Ireland, Morrison Chambers,
32 Nassau Street, Dublin D02 YH68, Ireland, https://eu-contact.penguin.ie.

Anna

More out of old habit than anything else, I watched Rick in the kitchen this morning, debating the precise moment to remind him. Too early and he'd wind up back in bed; too late and he'd still be a mess when I left the house. Some calculations you couldn't keep yourself from doing.

When I finally dropped the bomb—*Don't forget dinner tonight at Jen and Amir's*—he was halfway through his coffee, pacing back and forth behind the kitchen island. "Oh, *god*," he groaned, sinking onto a barstool, rubbing his face like he was trying to scrub away that reaction.

I waited.

"Oof, okay," he said finally, through his hands. "I just need to prepare myself." He looked up, his face childlike with worry. "You don't think *Samantha* will be there, do you?"

I resisted the reflex to reassure him, fearing some sarcasm would creep through, and told him, truthfully, that I didn't know. Then, to change the subject, I asked him how he was going to spend his day today. Four months into Rick's "indefinite hiatus," and both of us were running out of ideas.

I watched as he crossed his legs, one pale hairy flank appearing and disappearing from beneath his green robe. "First, I'm gonna answer some of those old sympathy notes, the ones we never got around to—"

"No one cares if you respond to those, Rick," I said gently.

He waved me off, sipping his coffee. "I know. Then I think I'll go running early, before it gets too hot. I did it yesterday. It felt really good, so I'm going to keep doing it. After that, I'll probably come back here and shower, then read for a few hours." He beheld me with distant amusement. "I guess that's it."

"Sounds good!" I said, trying to make my voice sound encouraging. "Maybe try and figure out a way to leave the house one more time before dinner. Oh, your book's upstairs on the dresser if you want it, by the way, and I saw your wallet. It's in the laundry room."

"Ah, thanks. The breadcrumb trail."

Rick got up and began making his haphazard rounds. I stayed in my chair. You had to be careful around him— his movements were so erratic and expansive that at any moment he was likely to wheel around and crash into you. I knew he was going to want his red shirt, which was in the dryer. I got up, fished it out, and waggled it at him. He did a little two-finger salute, pulled his old one off, and tossed it to me.

I put the dirty one to my face—another reflex—and was immediately rewarded with the impression of his chest hairs tickling my nose, the fruity musk of his armpit. It was such a potent memory that I teared up and threw the shirt roughly into the washing machine. Today was going to be long. I didn't have the luxury of getting emotional over laundry.

I watched as Rick sat on our entryway bench and worked one heel into a distressed sneaker with the thumb of the opposite hand, pausing in this ritual somehow to sip precariously from his coffee mug, which he then left behind on the bench en route to the door.

He paused, his hand on the knob. "Some days," he said, "I just want to die. Today is one of those days. I just want to die today. You know? Not coincidentally, I had three beers last night. I shouldn't tonight. Anyway, it's always good to see you in the morning."

"I love you. See you for dinner."

As soon as he was safely out the door, I got up to get dressed for my meeting. He hadn't asked what I was doing today, which meant I hadn't had to lie.

Small blessings.

Jen was the one who referred me to the lawyer. She'd taken pains to clarify, in an offhand way, that of course *she'd* never needed his services, but unspecified friends of hers in what she delicately referred to as my "situation" had apparently liked him very much. His demeanor was comforting. He didn't lay on any guilt trips. And of course, most important—a meaningful look here from Jen I tried to ignore—he had a reputation for getting his clients everything they *wanted*.

Despite all the sickening cloak-and-dagger involved in scheduling the meeting, I'd somehow forgotten it was this morning. When I remembered—around 4:00 a.m.—I'd almost bolted out of bed. Now I sat alone in the kitchen, calculating the route on my phone. The app said the drive would take about half an hour. I decided to give myself an hour. Ever since I disabled the car's AI, I've had to build extra time into every journey, to allow for getting lost and to give myself a few minutes to calm back down.

The streets around our house were quiet enough, mostly empty, so I felt pretty good starting out. I have to say, it really is like riding a bike—even after a decade-long break, the old instincts remain. I know I'll never be as good as the self-driving cars, which never drift or forget to signal. But I take some pride in muscle memory returning—stopping, leaning forward to check the intersection, turning hand over hand. It feels good, like Rick said, so I've kept doing it. I could just imagine his face if he knew, though: eyes bugged, arms waving, voice rising—something about a death wish, maybe.

I merged onto the highway and felt death encroaching. Cars shrieked past on both sides, the exit ramps peeling away and closing back in. Forty harrowing minutes later, I took my exit, parking hundreds of feet away from the other four cars. I fed myself a few dry almonds from the bag in the driver's-side door with shaky hands. I stared at the slice of my eyes in the rearview mirror for about five minutes until I was reasonably certain that no stranger could read distress into them.

Then I got out of the car.

The lawyer's building wasn't nice—whitewashed cinder block, swinging bulbs, stale air. There was something perfect about it, I decided. Where better, really, to find yourself sneaking around like this?

When I opened the office door, a youngish guy surprised me, striding from his desk with one hand extended, brushing his pants with the other. He apologized for the building— " 'Rathole' wouldn't be inaccurate," he said, laughing—and chattered on about new leases and upcoming renovations. I clocked his purple dress shirt, so creased and shiny he might've ripped the packaging open on it this morning. His haircut looked almost as new—Mormon? I found myself picturing his mother: Firm but kind. Crow's-feet from a lifetime's worth of indulgent smiles. She would've emphasized the importance of showing courtesy to middle-aged women.

Just as Jen promised, the lawyer was unfailingly, relentlessly pleasant. I wished he was meaner. Maybe, after all of my skulking around, I'd wanted a movie lawyer—sleazy, humiliating—to match my shame. This guy didn't even lose his warmth when confirming basic facts: "I've always wanted to live there myself, but my wife's work keeps us closer downtown," he remarked when I mentioned our neighborhood. I wondered what his wife did. The phrase "downtown" sounded exotic, like a relic from some earlier era.

He assured me that the first steps were always the most overwhelming. First of all, he had to know if I was "really committed" or not. "It's hard to get that ball rolling backward," he said, frowning with concern so pure I promised I wouldn't waste his time. I couldn't bear to watch that round face fall.

"No, no," he protested, genuinely alarmed at my uncharitable interpretation. As he cheerfully ran down the grim separation logistics, I found myself wondering how he'd gotten himself into this business. He wasn't some shark or a cold-blooded mercenary. He was a *softy*. I wanted to throw a blanket over his desk and hide under it with him, shining flashlights in each other's faces. I wanted to hurt him. I clenched my fists so hard I lost feeling in my fingertips.

Mercifully, the whole affair was over within an hour. Right before I left, he slid a fat pad and fearsome-looking silver pen across the desk and found my eyes. "Oh, and write everything down. All case notes on paper. Nothing digital."

When I asked him what he meant by "nothing digital," he just repeated himself, drawing the words out. My heart sank. Embarrassingly, I hadn't pictured this scenario involving homework.

"These things are personal," he added. "Assume everything is relevant. Often, the simplest and least significant thing a client imagines, something you didn't even really realize you'd written down, winds up making all the difference in negotiations."

"Negotiations." I hadn't really prepared myself for that word. What was I doing here? My head got swimmy, but I mastered it. I would *not* have a panic attack in front of this friendly kid in his brand-new purple dress shirt.

Instead, I smiled wide, thanked him profusely, took his hand with both of mine, made a self-deprecating joke about my degraded writing skills, and teased him about watering his plants. Then I made my slow way down the hall, listening with my whole body as the door handle latched behind me. Out in the parking lot, the configuration of the cars hadn't changed. Mine was farthest away. When I sat down at the steering wheel, I checked my eyes in the mirror again. They looked opaque, untroubled.

Out of curiosity, I tried crying. I hadn't been able to for three weeks now. As if in grudging response, my nervous system sent one tear, then two, sliding down, then no more. I held my outstretched palm in front of my face, then turned to pound the steering wheel—once, twice. Nothing, just a numbing jolt up my forearms. I gave up and stared at the blank legal pad on the passenger seat.

For legal reasons, I might be forced to journal. The irony was not lost on me, considering how many times a day Rick asked me, hopefully, how I was feeling. I'm not what people call an open book. Even Alex used to pester me about it.

He confronted me directly once, when he was fourteen. We were on the couch together, and he was showing me something he'd made in *UnWorld*. I was doing my best to pay attention as he moved some peculiar dog-faced beast around what seemed like a whimsically colored simulacrum of a farm, inviting me to appreciate the way the beast's jaws hinged open like a cartoon boa constrictor's to devour the pink rounded bits of cartoon fruit.

I couldn't find anything about the game that wasn't either ugly or bewildering, but I reminded myself that the school counselor had seen no issue with Alex's fixation: "It's a creative outlet for him, and it gets him out of that head," she'd said. Spending time in *UnWorld* seemed to help with his anxiety, so I said something encouraging: How clever that he'd managed to design it that way. Was it hard to do? Very, he'd said.

I was doing my best to feign interest when suddenly he looked up.

"Mom, why do you laugh like that?"

"Laugh like what?" I hadn't been aware of laughing.

"Like this," he said. Then he pantomimed my laugh— a silent, single *hee,* a gust of air like a sigh or a blown bike tire.

"I don't know," I answered, shifting slightly away on the couch. "I laugh like I laugh. I don't think you can choose something like that."

"I think you can," Alex had objected. "I like your laugh. But I think it's because of how you were raised."

"And what do you know about how I was raised?" I'd responded, trying to keep my voice light. I'd been subjected to a lot of psychoanalysis like this from him recently. Depending on the day and my mood, it felt either sweet or invasive, and we were in the latter territory.

"You were raised to be quiet, I think," he said. "I watch you with the other parents at school. Ellen's dad walked into you that one time, like you weren't even standing there. Remember?"

I didn't, I'd admitted. I guessed it was the kind of thing a son remembered seeing happen to his mother. I'd tried to brush him off, but his eyes were serious, intent.

"I want to hear what it sounds like when you laugh really loud," he'd said. "Like, throwing your head back. Here." He surged upward, abandoning the *UnWorld* screen, and proceeded to manipulate me like a department-store mannequin, kicking lightly at my feet to widen my stance and positioning my fists on my hips, superhero-style. Then he stepped back, examined his work for a minute, a grin on his face. "Okay, now give me your biggest belly laugh."

That was enough. I stuck my arms out straight like a zombie and pushed him onto the couch. "Can we go back to screen time now?" I said. "Or do I have to humiliate both of us by tickling you?"

His laugh, when it came, was bigger and warmer than my own.

"I'm serious, Mom," he said later, still smiling. "Take up some space."

I heard Rick in his voice, to be honest, and I wasn't sure I liked it. I waved a hand at him, *Enough, leave me be,* and told him to stop meddling in things he didn't understand.

So yes, I'm not famous for dwelling on my emotions. We can't all share everything. Some of us linger; some of us don't. I don't try arguing that my approach is superior, the way Rick does, even though he's never really been able to articulate the benefits of sharing everything.

Do I even have feelings? (A real thing Rick yelled, once, in a bad moment. I told him that question didn't feel great.) Sure. I get angry, sad, or hurt like everyone else. But I've always focused on the "like everyone else" half of that equation. Whenever I'm upset, I hear this voice in my head— I guess if we're insisting on psychoanalyzing, it's my mother's, no prizes there—asking: *And who are you, exactly?* It helps me. Why should I be the one taking up all the attention, if we all need it? "Unflappable," my mom called me, approvingly. I didn't know what the word meant as a kid, except I knew it was a compliment and that the opposite must be silly, like a big, panicked bird, beating its stupid wings all over everybody.

Like Rick.

The lawyer's office was located in the middle of nowhere: just a bunch of warehouse spaces around me, all of which I assumed were automated. Which meant I faced three empty hours with nothing much to do, no errands to run, and—thanks to Jen and Amir—no dinner to prepare. I started the car and drove cautiously down a few pitted, sunken streets until I came across a desolate-looking sandwich spot. A few humans in there, although it definitely wasn't the kind of place where you wanted to dine in.

I did it anyway. I sat at the window, which faced only the parking lot and the highway entrance, chewing slowly.

I tried to make the whole experience stretch out as long as I could by watching a crane dangle a blue shipping container high on the horizon, slightly darker than the sky behind it. One of Alex's anxieties involved never passing anywhere near one of these cranes. Just seeing them in the distance, like this, was enough. He would turn his head and squeeze his eyes shut, like someone waiting for a ride to be over.

I didn't tell him what I knew, which was that there were once humans involved at every level of this perilous task. Men and women once operated these machines, often getting their limbs pulped or shredded in spectacularly grisly fashion in the process. The few construction accidents I'd witnessed decades ago in the Emergency Department lingered uncomfortably in my memory.

I gazed with sudden distaste at the remains of my sandwich and found myself bored by the mathematical certainty that the shipping container would reach its destination safely and without incident. I balled up the remaining bits, threw them away, and left.

It's been really difficult having this much time to kill. Once, my days were filled with pressing checklist items—clothes or shoes to buy, conflicting appointments to navigate, swimming or piano lessons—but now there's nothing but oceans of time, and no matter how I busy myself, I simply cannot manage to fill it. Having my hands so completely free—my laundry done, folded, and put away, every task I could imagine already checked off—has been humiliating in a way I can't quite put my finger on. What's more shameful than an adult with too much time on her hands?

I took the longest way home I could find, taking an exit three stops away and almost getting lost finding my way back. I went slowly, watching the streets thin out and the houses get prettier. Rick's car was parked in the driveway, but when I went into the house and called out, no one answered, so I ran upstairs to get changed. I would do my makeup in the mirror in the bathroom and then drive back over to Jen and Amir's. With all this back-and-forth, shuttling myself from one place to another, the day almost seemed busy.

Going through my closet, I settled on a backless dress I hadn't dared wear in a few years—why not, I figured— and shoes with a modest heel. The outfit seemed to gain momentum on its own. I spent a little extra time on my makeup, fished out some dangly earrings, and accentuated it all with the brass necklace Rick bought me for our ten-year anniversary. I couldn't remember the last time I put on two nice outfits in one day.

I left again a little on the early side, parking a few cars back instead of in Jen and Amir's driveway. It was a courtesy thing; I was early enough that if I walked over to the house, they would have to invite me in alone, maybe while they were still getting things together. I didn't want to make the situation any more awkward than it already promised to be.

I also didn't relish standing around out here, halfway between my house and theirs. If they looked out the window and saw me all dressed up, looking lost on the sidewalk, that would be worse. Jen would have to come out and retrieve me, coax me into the house like I was some kind of stray. I looked around. Waiting in the car seemed like a bad idea, too. Shifty, somehow. I didn't want Rick to walk right past our car and spot me huddled in front of the wheel on a warm night.

I settled for getting out and taking a walk around the block, thinking that I might bump into Rick. I didn't see anyone out as I made one last loop.

About two blocks ahead of me, I spotted Rick, unmistakable with his skinny shoulders and brisk, abstracted walk. I didn't quite know how we'd missed each other in the house, or how he'd even spent his day. But here he was, wearing an unbuttoned heather-gray dress shirt over his red tee, and I could tell that he saw me, too, by the way his walk slowed down and opened up. I was still about two hundred feet away when he called, "Hey, there," his voice oddly clear even at this distance. We kept walking toward each other until we met in front of someone's house. His stubble had started going white around his chin. He looked nice tonight.

"Your glasses are smudged," I told him. He took off his blocky aviators and polished them on his T-shirt, popping them back on and blinking at me theatrically.

"Better," I said. I watched his face as he registered my appearance, and he grinned in sincere appreciation.

"You look *beautiful*," he said.

"Thank you." I laughed. "Embarrassing, how dressed up I got just to go down the block."

"I haven't seen that dress in a long time," he said, taking

a step back to admire me in it. I felt a little warmth spread through my body despite the chill of the air on my exposed back.

"Come here," I said, taking his hand.

He looked at me, and then, instead of asking me about my day, or how I was, just asked, "Ready?"

Some grateful admiration, still, for my Rick. Which of course brought with it a rush of guilt as I looked into his eyes. He wasn't hiding anything.

It wasn't until we stood outside Jen and Amir's house that I felt it in my stomach. We hadn't seen Jen in any capacity for a couple months, Amir for even longer. We'd stayed away from them, and from the house, and now it seemed more powerful, somehow—looming. The light of the city was visible, like it always was, just a faint glow from behind the trees.

"How do you think it's going to be?" I asked.

"Weird," Rick said. "I'm sure it'll be weird."

We both looked at the top floor. Samantha's room light was off.

"Do you think she's there?" he asked.

Before either of us could answer, the door swung open, and Jen surged forward, waving both hands over her head. Hello, you, she cooed, pulling me in for an embrace, her pixie cut tickling my cheek. Her grip was fierce enough to constrict my breathing, bringing tears to my eyes. When she pulled back, she caught me wiping them away and misjudged, clucking sympathetically.

Before I could clarify that I hadn't been crying, that in

fact crying had become *impossible,* Amir wandered out, rubbing his bald head and squinting as if ducking beneath an invisible doorframe. He reached out to take Rick's hand in both of his and uttered his name, *Rick,* with a strange kind of finality, before turning and inviting us to follow him in for drinks. Rick shot me a bewildered look. I looked down to hide my smile.

Walking inside, I realized I'd rehearsed our initial meeting so long I'd forgotten to worry about reentering their house. How many more blindingly obvious things would take me aback today?

To be fair, Sam and Alex had spent a lot less time together here. There were fewer memories in this house to trip me up. Ever since the day she first showed up with Alex at our door, age ten—"I thought I'd walk him home, because he's eight," she announced, the rebuke implicit in her voice— Sam had always preferred to come over to us.

It was difficult to see what they shared at first, this earnest, solemn older girl and our happy, strange little boy, except for loneliness and each other. But the more time they spent together, the more I saw they rhymed: both dark-haired only children, both carrying themselves with a certain remove. One sullen, one serene. Sam threw herself into Alex's little-boy pretend games with a touching sincerity, like they were something important she'd forgotten to do. Like they were sacred rites.

And now, there they were, right in front of me, splayed out on Jen and Amir's beige sectional like two creatures without skeletal systems. I could see them: Alex on his back, facing away, only his curls visible above the arm of the couch, raising corn chips to his mouth from a wooden bowl. Sam in the opposite corner, her feet tucked beneath her, their toes just touching, reading some bizarre factoid from her phone Alex had just asked her to look up. I could practically smell him—earthy, warm, slightly sour. Like Rick's shirt this morning.

Not here, I told myself. There was nothing in the world I wanted more, standing in their foyer, than *not* to make a scene in front of Jen and Amir. All we had to do was get back home, and then I could have whatever nervous breakdown I wanted. Somewhere safe, away from the pitying gazes of these two. I walked in and chose the corner of the couch where Alex's imaginary curly mop had been and sat down on it. We would fucking get through this.

Then I felt Rick's absence and turned to find him still in the doorway. He was sobbing.

"I'm sorry," he said, his voice cracking. "It's just hard to be back in here for the first time."

He turned his head and waved a hand. As I watched Rick be encircled by Amir with a stiff-armed caress, Jen leaving the couch to hug him in one smooth, fluid motion, I had only one thought: *Please stop.* He was making a mess.

Finally, Rick sat on the couch next to me, letting out a showy breath and a self-conscious laugh. "Okay," he said, "sorry, guys, not a great start." He reached over and took my hand. Every muscle in my body tightened. I tried to squeeze it back without conveying my irritation.

This makes me sound heartless. I don't mean to be. Rick—and I know this to be 100 percent true—never actually tries to siphon attention away from me. He just does it, easy as drawing air. Maybe it's my thin mouth, but no one ever stops me to ask, unprompted, how I'm feeling today, which is something people seem to ask Rick on a near-daily basis. But I wouldn't really want people doing that. Would I? And wasn't the fact that he understood me, without my needing to explain myself, what I loved most about Rick?

Still, some unreasonable part of me felt diminished as Rick calmed down. Like we'd soiled the rug. Amir broke the silence, announcing he was making drinks for whoever wanted them. Relieved, we all said some version of *Right here, Yes please, Sign me up.*

Then Jen turned her attention to me. She told me how wonderful I looked, touched my back, and gently pelted me with a long stream of questions, all without pausing for answers—How are you guys doing, hon? How's things? How's the hospital?

I'd forgotten how good Jen was at simulating the act of listening. She said "Mmm-hmmm" in a throaty murmur as you talked, laughed appreciatively and often. I knew that it was a trick—the sleepy, conspiratorial edge to her voice, the twinkle in her eyes that grew doll-like the closer you looked—but I couldn't deny it felt nice. As we chatted, I inspected Jen's cool blue eyes, wondering: Was Samantha being kept from us? Protected, maybe? Or were we being shielded from her?

On the easy chair in a far corner, I could see the checkered throw blanket that I usually only saw crumpled up at Samantha's feet. It was folded neatly, which would suggest she was out somewhere.

"So where's Samantha tonight," I asked, and I thought I detected a moment's hesitation before Jen responded.

"Oh, honey, you know she doesn't tell me, at least not in a language I speak. Just 'out,' which I'm pretty sure means 'alone.' I almost wish she were getting into regular-kid trouble. Then, I'd at least know what to say." She sighed, then brightened. "She did promise that she'd try to pop in before dinner ended. She didn't want to miss seeing you."

Before I could ask more questions about Sam, Amir wandered over with four reddish-brown drinks. Music had started—something with a twangy guitar sound and an insistent voice singing above it, not in English.

We chatted for a while about nothing much—Jen's work, her caseload. She was so self-deprecating about her corporate law work she wouldn't even say the words without an eye roll. "I serve no purpose to anyone," she liked to say.

I told her a brief, half-hearted story about the asshole doctor I always complained about, and Jen shook her head and laughed. "So there's really no human staff anywhere else in the hospital?"

"They've overstated the case a little," I told her—the drink numbed my lips. "People still want us around when they're in real trouble." But there's no denying the building feels emptier these days, I added. The floor I really didn't like to visit was Geriatric Long Term. There was no one else there but the patients. You would walk past all these poor souls who didn't always have the greatest grip on reality anymore anyway, and they were just surrounded by . . . equipment. No faces to gaze into, nobody there to calm them.

"I mean, it's strange," I said. "Technically, their medical needs are being met, in some cases better than if we were there. But there's something so depressing about it."

"They've done studies," Amir chimed in from the kitchen as he pulled down water glasses from a cupboard. "Regarding the success rate of human care versus non-staffed floors."

I waited for him to keep going. "And?"

He flashed me a solicitous smile, all four glasses nested awkwardly in his arms. "There's no contest, really," he said. "The care on the AI-staffed floors is, on average, much better. It's crystal clear from the data. With all-human staff, the rate of complications, infections, bad outcomes"—as he enumerated this dire list, he set down each glass on the stone table with a bang—*"skyrockets."*

Jen let out an awkward laugh while Rick fixed me with a pretend-perplexed look. "Did you hear that, honey? Skyrockets."

That made everyone laugh—even Amir, who held up his hands, protesting that we didn't let him finish. Unfortunately, the depression rates were catastrophic on the AI-staffed floors, he said. "I guess it all comes down to what you believe is important."

"People still crave the laying on of hands," I said, holding mine up and fluttering my fingers as if they proved something—the existence of hands. There was the potential for suggestiveness in my words, I realized, but no one reached for the obvious dirty joke, because no one thought of me this way.

Instead, Jen asked, "Anna, your mother was in palliative care, right?"

"It's true," I said, startled by her memory. In my mind's eye, a flash of my mother's daily lipstick, inexpertly applied by her live-in aide, as she took her final, shuddering breaths. I looked at Jen, not sure when I would have shared this bit of my own life and wondering at the fact she'd retained it. Clearly, she'd been listening, so here she was, bringing it back to me. A token of friendship, a reminder of the time we'd shared together. Why did it feel like a house cat depositing the entrails from its catch next to my shoes?

The talk continued, but something was off. Maybe it had been Rick's outburst, but we couldn't find our footing. Rick started asking Amir work questions, even though Amir does something in AI that neither Rick nor I understand well and that Amir isn't prone to talking about. Usually, when we asked, he would just grimace politely and say it had to do with the way that systems talked to one another, now that there were so many more opportunities for miscommunication. Rick and I both laughed at the thought of Amir—a guy prone to long, uncomfortable silences—in charge of helping systems communicate.

I looked around. Jen and Amir always seemed to have more of some essential quality—money, certainly, or maybe just poise, or maybe poise was the same thing as money, and I just couldn't see it. Everything in their house was either rigorously symmetrical or just slightly asymmetrical enough to draw your attention. As we talked, I found myself staring at an orange metallic cow skull, about the size of a muskrat's head, balanced on top of a stack of books across from me. Why was it there? Who would want such a thing in their house? The music had a bright, steely edge that I suddenly needed to get away from.

That's when the drink hit me. I felt unsteady, like I needed to get up but also like I didn't trust myself. I tried to distract myself by imagining the flight of steps up to Sam's room. I could see my feet walk up the stairs, but things got cloudy at the top. Like there was something waiting at the landing, blocking my way and unwilling to let me see more.

The more I tried focusing, the more disoriented I felt, like maybe the entire house was disassembling itself around me. I fought a sudden impulse to stand up, walk upstairs, push right through that dark cloud, open Samantha's door, and . . . what?

I realized—from Rick's and Jen's and Amir's looks of mild surprise—that I *had* stood up, with no clear signal that I was heading anywhere. Whoops. I apologized and veered, ignoring Rick's questioning eyes and heading not for the stairs leading up to Samantha's room but to the kitchen to fill up a glass of water. Behind me, Jen's and Rick's voices poured into the gap my absence created as I tried to regroup, focusing on the hiss of the tap.

By the time I sat back down, the chitchat had shifted, and I found that Jen was talking about how much her upload had planned the night.

Jen liked to go on about all the things her upload helped her with—she had been the first person I'd ever met with one, and their synchronicity was deep and impressive. Before being introduced to hers, uploads had struck me as remote, a strange extravagance for narcissistic rich people, the equivalent of owning commercial spacecraft. Jen and Amir had more money than we did, sure, and their house was much bigger than ours. But they weren't, you know, *rich;* just our regular, slightly more-well-off neighbors.

Jen was going on about how the upload coordinated the music, ordered the groceries, kept track of the timing of the cooking. For her, the upload was a convenience. It's obscene, she was saying. I hardly do anything anymore. I would feel guilty, if I didn't know better.

"What do you mean, *know* better?"

There must have been something in my voice. Usually, I waited for a pause in the conversation, but Jen immediately broke off and looked at me. "I just mean that the upload has so much processing capacity, it hardly notices when it's doing low-level menial tasks," she said evenly. "Or at least, isn't that what you told me, Amir?"

Amir gave a cool smile and nodded. Menial tasks ran on the equivalent of the upload's autonomic nervous system, he said. In other words, they "cost" as much, in cognitive terms, as blinking. The little tasks we struggled to complete in our daily lives lay so far beneath the upload's "awareness" that you couldn't really say they were being conscripted into labor or asked to focus on things they didn't "want" to focus on. "I have a lot of theories on this idea of uploads 'wanting' anything, anyway," Amir said, "but that's a whole other topic."

"Actually, I'm very interested in that," I said. "I'd love to hear your theories."

He looked at me, a little surprised. "I think I'd say, without getting too deep in the weeds," he said, "that humans like to see themselves reflected in their gadgets, their technologies. If you want to see something badly enough, you're bound to find it."

This was very Amir—curt, cryptic, seemingly diplomatic, somehow condescending. Jen's expression didn't crack, but I noticed her shift position on the sofa. Rick reached for my knee with an urgency I couldn't decipher: Was that a comforting hand or a warning?

The drink, I saw, seemed to have made Rick gabbier. He was talking, laughing, cheeks flushed. I snuck glances at him while Jen filled our balloon glasses. He'd been crying in the doorway less than twenty minutes earlier, but now he looked healthier than I'd seen him in months.

Usually, this touched me—his eagerness to push conversation like a ball around the room, his tendency to blossom in any room with at least one woman in it.

Why was I angry now, then? He was helping. He'd sensed my energy flagging, so he swooped in to keep the conversation going, to get us through this together. I opened my mouth to laugh at what he said. I tried to drown out the ugly little voice inside that muttered: *Must be so easy.*

We sat down to dinner. Amir carved the roast with joyless precision and focus, passing slivers of meat along on white plates. The roast was slightly pink, the center of the perfectly rounded medallions like a slapped cheek. I tasted the wine, feeling the warmth bloom inside my mouth. Good wine, good things. I felt light, inconsequential, like

I was being moved along in a wide river. I found myself struggling to hold the thread of conversation.

"Did you ever go back to Mexico again, Amir?" Rick said.

"He turned out to be a real wimp," Jen said, then quoted someone—a colleague, maybe—on her disappointing boy-friend. " 'The kind of guy who won't even pee straight into the toilet because it's too loud,' she called him. That cracked me up."

"It's the way he makes the coffee," Amir said. "Two scoops, five cups. Anything more and it's bilge."

"Abso-lutely incredible prose," Rick said. "Cold to the touch, like a metal table. Even you liked it, right, Anna? Well, I don't mean *even*. But you liked it, right?"

I nodded, unsure of what he or anyone was talking about. No one had mentioned Alex. I was starting to have a sliding sensation, like the house was pitching sideways. I could feel Rick catching my eye, attempting to check in with me, but I seemed to have lost my voice. Whatever agency I had was slipping away like smoke into vents.

If only I had remembered the damn lawyer's meeting sooner, I could've contrived some reason for us to resched-ule. Or cancel. I was contemplating how we might end the evening prematurely when I heard the doorknob turn behind me.

Jen's face lit up. You're here, you're right on time, we've all had too much to drink, there's plenty left over, she called over my shoulder, all at once and in a strangely musical register, as if transmitting a coded message.

Hairs rose on my neck as Samantha's physical presence established itself behind me.

As Jen rose to greet her daughter, I stood up unexpectedly for the second time that night. Jen faltered, so it was me who was first to turn and greet Samantha.

I had been wondering why I had consented to Jen's badgering, buttonholed into our first night out in months. Now I was certain that I'd been desperate to lay eyes on Samantha. This meeting was the reason we were here.

I froze when I saw her. Normally, Sam was inscrutable, her jungle-cat eyes transmitting perfect indifference. Her stare was so flattening that Rick had joked it made him want to rattle spoons, clear his throat, knock over books. "Just to prove I still exist," he said. Unlike her mother's eyes, Sam's carried no light, no false promises of intimacy. Jen and Amir had nicknamed her the Sphinx.

Tonight, however, her eyes were red and streaming, and to my astonishment, she clutched me when I reached her, as if she were afraid of falling, and began coughing out hard, ugly sobs into my shoulder. My arms flew around her as much to reciprocate as to steady myself, and I heard Jen's voice splintering behind me, Amir's chair scraping. As I patted her, murmuring, a dim recollection came of another, similar time—Sam sobbing, her face in my arm, repeating, I'm sorry, I'm sorry; my arm, just like this, offering limp comfort. Jen, maybe somewhere nearby, importuning Sam to turn around, come away.

Had this happened and, if so, when? I couldn't be sure.

For months, I'd been stumbling across holes in my mind, dropping things that should be there.

Sam pulled herself away and wiped her eyes, one tear-drop falling and immediately disappearing in the air. Jen, Amir, and Rick wavered behind us, united in uselessness and unsure whether to intervene, as I braced for what Sam might be about to tell me, the revelation that had sent her stumbling through the door.

"Nice dress," she said.

"I—thank you," I said.

She gazed around at the adults behind us, as if noticing we weren't alone for the first time. "Hi, everyone," she said, vaguely. "I'm sorry to disrupt things. Are you all having a nice evening?"

"Honey, what *happened* to you?" asked Jen.

"Nothing, Mom." Suddenly she was as placid as she'd sounded inconsolable, just seconds earlier. "I was just—you know, thinking. Nothing wrong with that, right?"

She turned to me. Such strange formality to her, like you were simultaneously being mocked and placated. "I don't actually intend to stay, Anna, and I'm sorry for the whole production here." Gesturing to herself, her own tearstained face. "I've been having, you know, a bit of a weird time of it lately. But I had to come and say something to you."

"Sam, what is this about?" Amir sounded angrily uncertain, like he couldn't decide exactly who needed to be protected or disciplined in this developing situation.

"Sam, honey," Jen cut in, "you're upset. Why don't you go upstairs, take a moment, decompress, then come down again. We'll clear the plates, and you can join us for dessert."

Sam shot her parents a look of devastating coldness. "No, thank you, I'm fine." Her eyes returned to me. "I know we haven't talked for a while, Anna, and first of all I'm sorry for that. I've been trying to unscramble some things in my mind. I wanted you to know that tonight I came to the definitive conclusion: Alex didn't mean to do it."

"Sam," Jen cut in, severe. "This isn't the time or the place. Please don't—"

"Whatever happened to him," she continued, "it was at least partially an accident. He would never have done that to me, or to you."

"Come sit down, please, the both of you," pleaded Amir.

Why couldn't they shut up, the both of them? We needed to be alone, Sam and me. I tried to tell her with my eyes that, to me, we were.

"Something happened to him," Sam continued, leaning forward. "I don't know what it is yet, or what it means. But I've been thinking about his behavior the week before. He was whispering and whistling a lot, humming little songs under his breath, recording them. I don't know what they mean, but they might—"

Suddenly, she stopped. Her eyes unfocused again, and she seemed confused. I wanted to grab her, shake her back into herself. *What?* My mouth formed the words, but I couldn't get them out. *Might be what?*

But somehow it was too late, as if a bubble had popped, or a hypnotist had clapped. "I'm . . . I'm not sure," she said, giving me a pleading look. "Maybe I'm wrong?"

Whatever she was going to say next, she didn't get to. Jen wedged herself between us. "Let's get you upstairs," Jen said gently, reaching for Sam's elbow as if she were frail and sick.

"I don't understand," Sam said, looking even more confused, backing slightly away from her mother, and from me. I couldn't tell whom she was addressing, or what she meant. But when Jen reached for Sam's elbow again, Sam let her take it.

She was about to be led away when Sam roused herself, found my eyes again, and said flatly, "I'm sorry to upset you. I've had a hard time telling things apart recently." She pulled away from Jen's grip but only to trudge up the steps by herself, pausing on the second stair.

"Whatever it is he wanted, I don't think he got it," she said.

Then she disappeared.

I became aware of Jen standing next to me in the stricken silence, leaning into Amir, who had wrapped his arms around her. Rick was still at the table, looking pale. Desperate, I tried to follow the rhythm of Sam's black combat boots up to her room in my mind, but the dark cloud that had blocked my view earlier was still there, and she was swallowed up in it. By the time her bedroom door shut, I was completely alone.

"I'm so, so sorry," Jen broke in. "She's been having these . . . moments . . . lately. Episodes? We're not sure." She paused.

"It's been difficult," she said, more quietly. "You know how she is. We want to help, but whenever we try to reach out, we just can't find a way in, you know?" Helpless, she clawed the air in front of her, as if she were struggling with a jar lid or wringing a neck. Then she dropped her arms. "She comes, she goes. I try to give space. I'm not great at it."

"I have to confess, guys," Amir chimed in. "I wasn't sure how she was going to be tonight. I suggested she stay away for a while because I thought she might upset you." He shrugged. "Turns out I was right."

Jen looked as defeated as I'd ever seen her. I sensed Rick and Amir waiting for me to console her, but I found I couldn't do it. God help me, I looked at those deep worry lines and felt envy—the marks of a mother who still had the luxury of worrying about her still-alive child.

Together we murmured our concerns, asked the questions—yes, counseling at least once a week, Amir assured us—but even as I put my hand on Jen's sinewy shoulder, my mind remained riveted on the second floor, trying to sense whatever cloudy thoughts and feelings Samantha was having up there. If there'd been some natural way to contrive a reason to follow her, I would have. But there was no way to do it without frightening everybody.

I turned to Rick, hoping to catch his eye. Surely he sensed how badly I needed to talk to her? *Say something,* I begged silently. We both knew that if Rick demanded to go up and talk to Sam, everyone would reorganize themselves around his needs. Because that's what everyone always did.

Instead, he flashed an apologetic smile. "I think maybe we've all had enough for one night," he said. "Still a little rough around the edges."

At this suggestion that the night might be ending, Jen's

composure returned instantly. As we gathered our things, Alex's voice elbowed its way into my head—*You're quiet.*

Alex tended to leave everything in his path slightly askew: rugs kicked out of alignment, sheets bunched, one glass left on a window ledge. It was like he was leaving a trail to follow, little disturbances marking his progress through the world. He had spent so much time in this house. And yet as I looked around at Jen and Amir's immaculate house again, I couldn't see a trace of him.

Nothing here was out of place.

A horrible thought came to me: Maybe Alex was just an idea that we had. Somehow I had blinked or lost track of him, and now we couldn't prove he had ever existed. This was the final violence of death: It turned people back into ideas.

Somehow, Rick and I found ourselves outside, Jen and Amir standing in the doorway. Jen stood in front of me. Now her eyes had turned into a perimeter fence. I didn't know what kind of territory lay behind them. Whatever it looked like, I wasn't sure I'd ever existed there. Had Alex?

Amir perked back up, too, repeating how good it was to see us, how often they thought of us. His arm clasped on his wife's shoulder, squinting his smile at me, the two of them arrayed against us. With their daughter shut up safely behind them, I suspected that if they never saw the two of us again, they would feel nothing but relief.

Alone again together on the sidewalk, Rick and I walked for a minute before he broke the silence.

"Fuck," he said, half to me, half to himself. "I'd been wondering if Jen and Amir were doing enough for her. Clearly, they aren't. She seems pretty acute, still."

He went on about Samantha and Amir and Jen and the dinner, about how complicated it all was. I nodded, not listening and thinking of nothing but Samantha's gaze.

The animal panic in her eyes burned a hole in me; I'd been unable to hear what they were saying. She'd gone up to her room on her own, but somehow it seemed like I'd watched her get dragged away by hospital orderlies. Like some conspiracy had formed itself to keep us apart.

And Rick. He'd been a part of that conspiracy. He'd stayed at the table, watching Jen pry us apart, and did nothing. Said *nothing*. Had he really been that oblivious to my panic? I had trouble believing it. Not Mr. Empathy. Not my walking lie detector. I kept my eyes on the sidewalk, because if I turned around, I didn't trust myself not to run back to the house.

Up ahead, I saw the car and quickened my steps. Suddenly, I needed to put space between myself and the relentless sound of Rick's voice. I turned to him.

"I'm driving," I said.

It wasn't always easy to stop Rick, but he broke off, attempting to suss out whether or not I was joking. Seeing my seriousness, his eyes widened—shock, some mild interest. "Seriously?"

"I have been. For three weeks."

A pregnant pause passed between us. I couldn't really see his eyes. Then, a disbelieving laugh. "Wow. I haven't driven a car in ten years. How does it feel?"

There was awe in his voice. In spite of everything, I smiled. "Honestly? Terrifying. I must be losing my mind. Come on, get in—maybe the secret is to get a few drinks in me first."

Our eyes met over the hood. For a moment I saw a faint spark of the boyishness that had pulled me toward him. No matter how gray his hair got, there was always something childlike about Rick—the way he pulled his legs up underneath him when he sat on the couch, the way his tongue protruded slightly when he focused.

Now, he slapped the hood and let out a giggle. "I am but a humble passenger," he proclaimed, taking his seat and reaching for his belt with an exaggerated enthusiasm. "In your will, my peace."

As I pulled away, executing a careful little K-turn and nosing my way down the block, I could feel him still smiling at me. "I forgot how many things you are better at than I am," he said quietly.

We fell into a silence that stretched out a little too long as the trip continued.

"She looked older," Rick said finally. "Different, somehow."

"I noticed that, too." I paused. "Four months can be a long time in a teenager's life."

"It was disturbing, seeing her like that," Rick said. "She didn't even seem to know what was going on. I hope Jen and Amir are taking it seriously."

As we neared the highway, the houses gave way to weedy lots and a glowing emptiness that matched the inside of my head. "Rick, I think she needed to tell us something. She never got to finish."

Rick made a noise with one nostril—not as unkind as snorting, but not far removed. "I don't think she had anything to say. She wasn't making sense."

Something in the hardness of his tone bothered me. "You didn't see. I was right next to her. She looked desperate. Then Jen and Amir swooped in. Didn't you get the feeling they were trying to keep us apart?"

"I think they just wanted to get her out of our sight as soon as possible when they saw how upset she was," Rick said. "Get back to business as usual. You know how they are."

"Maybe we should invite Sam over." I cast a glance at him. "Just the three of us. She might feel more comfortable talking about . . . about what happened that night."

Rick shifted away, his whole body tense. When he finally spoke, his voice came out perfectly calm. "I don't think that would be a good idea."

"Why?"

He turned to look at me, perturbed. "Anna, what on earth about Sam's behavior tonight suggested that spending time with us would be *good* for her? She barged in, had a panic attack, and ran away. Do you really think she needs us prying into her trauma? No, what she most needs from us is space."

Evidently, this was the story Rick had decided to tell himself. By refusing to look at Sam, by failing to even say hello to her tonight, by switching subjects anytime I brought her up, he was somehow protecting *Samantha,* looking out for her mental health. Which I was in danger of violating. Of course.

"I didn't like the way she looked, walking up the stairs," I tried again. "She looked resigned. She's usually so"—I struggled to find the proper word for Samantha, whose limpid gaze and matter-of-fact observations sometimes made you feel like one of you was an alien, or both of you were—"not like that. It was like she'd been lobotomized. Wouldn't you have a hard time being forthright with Jen and Amir around? They seemed determined to pretend Alex never existed. We might be able to help her."

I waited. Nothing.

"She *likes* us, Rick."

He took a long breath in and out. "Sam's mental health isn't our responsibility right now. We have all we can do to look after ourselves."

"'I don't think he got what he wanted.' Is that what she said? Rick, don't you want to know what she meant?"

"I have no *idea* what she meant, Anna," he said, shaping the phrase into an aggrieved little schoolteacher's melody. "But I know that you're not going to get answers from a traumatized kid who watched her best friend die."

"So that's your response to everything we saw tonight? To do *nothing*?"

"I think we should leave it alone," he said flatly. I snuck another glance at him. His face was hard, stone, unfeeling. "I think you should leave her alone."

Everyone always told me how they envied my emotionally available partner—so empathic, so intuitive. "I'm jealous of the way Rick dotes on you," Jen had once told me, in a rare nonbulletproof moment. "Amir can be so cold."

But what no one else seemed to notice—except me, of course, which never failed to make me feel small and ungrateful—was the way Rick's considerations for other people usually wound up looking a lot like whatever Rick was already doing for himself. He wasn't just kind—he was *vehemently* kind, a vehemence which masked a submerged hostility, an anger toward everyone and everything. Once you noticed it you began to suspect even his most solicitous gestures.

Rick frequently begged me to open up more, often with an infinite weariness suggesting that my emotional tone-deafness had grown too burdensome. And yet when I did open up, he often grew startled and angry, particularly if my answer diverged from his expectations. Rick loved guessing what I was feeling, but he didn't exactly love hearing he'd been wrong. I had just finished telling him something I needed, after all, and he had feigned his own deafness in response.

Or had he? Perhaps I hadn't used the right words, the ones he would somehow need me to use in order for him to understand. This proved the pointlessness of words to me—even if you told people exactly what you felt, they could make it mean anything they wanted in their heads. They could even (and often did) turn them against you. Why bother?

I moved onto the ramp and eyed the column of cars moving along the highway, then pressed the gas, and the car floated into the middle lane. "You just don't want to see her, do you?" I said. I watched my knuckles whiten on the steering wheel and heard Rick's sharp intake of breath, although what it was in response to I didn't know. "Sometimes I get the feeling that you'd actually be happy if you never saw Sam ever again."

"Look, fucking *yes*, I would," Rick exploded. His voice was pinched, and his hands were bunching in his lap. "I don't particularly want to see her again, okay? Seeing Samantha's face does not give me joy. It's unpleasant. *She's* unpleasant. She stares right through me with those fucking animal eyes, she ignores every attempt to get to know her, and the night Alex died, she was the only one with him. So yeah. How am I supposed to feel? She's not my kid, you know? Now that Alex is gone, I don't necessarily have to care about her."

"Apart from you and me, Rick, she knew Alex better than anyone," I said quietly.

Rick waved a hand wildly over his head. "I can't, I *can't*," he said, his voice rising. "I can't go into that space. What if she did something to him? She could hardly give a straight answer about that night. She said he just walked up to the edge and fell over. How do we know she wasn't doing something dangerous, or asking him to do something? Hell, she always seemed slightly disturbed. How do we know she wasn't the one trying to jump, and he fell trying to stop her?"

"*Rick,*" I said, and he shook his head at the shock and disgust in my voice.

"This is why I can't go there," he said. "I just can't, okay, Anna?" He paused, collecting himself, and when he spoke, his voice came out even, measured, somehow still passive-aggressive.

"Seeing her is upsetting, and I'm trying to keep myself from spiraling out here," he said carefully. "I'm protecting myself. Isn't that okay to be doing?"

"Yes, sure, fine," I said. "Protect yourself." Then, because the drinks had loosened my grip; because I could feel the blood racing down my arms; and because, fuck it, why not at this point: "God forbid anything intervenes between you and your self-*protection*."

I felt Rick retreating to the quietly dignified sulk he adopted whenever I dared express anger.

"I actually need to protect myself a lot around you," he said, huffily. "Not that you'd notice. When your partner clams up and yells about everything except what's actually bothering her, the air gets a little suffocating."

"Saint Rick," I sneered. I mean, he clearly wanted to take the gloves off. "Okay, let me ask you this, because I'm genuinely curious. Have you ever, in our marriage, cast yourself as the bad guy? I beg you to tell me one situation, if you can, where you were certain you were in the wrong. Because what are the chances, right? There's one guy in history, he's right one hundred percent of the time, and that one guy is you?" I eased into the fast lane, and didn't deny myself the pleasure of noting Rick's visible discomfort as I rounded seventy-five. "What does that make me, in your eyes? Imagine if I *were* as wretched as you imagine me." I'd gotten a little tangled up in that last one, but it must've hit its target, because Rick deflated.

"Look, I know you're handling things better than I've

been," he said heavily. "You're already back at work, you're helping people, you're part of all this—this *effort*. I've got nothing. I'm doing nothing. You don't need to rub my nose in it. Trust me, I do it enough." He fell silent, gazing out the window. I was just about to reach for his hand.

"But at least I don't make you figure it all out *for* me," he said suddenly, his voice rising as his mind caught the edge of his argument again. I took my hand away. "Living with you and your unprocessed emotions? It's like having a third person in the marriage. It doesn't leave a lot of room for me."

"You're home! Every day! Wallowing in your processed emotions! You're practically fucking *pickled* in them, Rick. And what good has it done you? Would you like to share with me the great insight that ruminating every day in your bathrobe for months has gained you, while I work twelve-hour shifts standing on my feet, making us money?"

Rick withdrew, once more, into silence—punishing me, I suppose. Now I was being treated to his disappearing trick, where he traveled a million miles away from me without moving. But what could I say? I had crossed the line into insults. I'd brought up money, my job, his work. A low blow. He was a *schoolteacher*, for Christ's sake. As if he could walk back in there. The frightened eyes of students, the whispers of teachers. I could never.

"I'm sorry I brought up the money," I muttered, and he simply nodded. Oh, how wounded, how noble in his doleful bearing, was my Rick. Somehow, I'd lost again.

Just then, I saw that our exit was about to pass on the right.

I wrenched the wheel across three lanes of traffic.

"Fuck! Jesus! Anna!" Rick yelped. No honking, no swerving—the driverless cars just parted, soundlessly.

When we got home, Rick reached behind him to pull off his loafers, like a tired woman taking off stilettos. We flashed each other weak smiles of apology, in accordance with our long-held rule about not going to bed mad, and after touching my back briefly, he padded upstairs without a word.

I didn't feel like following him, so I went outside and sat on the patio. It was unseasonably chilly for spring. I shivered in my dress, but instead of going inside, I sat down on the concrete square outside the sliding glass doors, the cold grit biting into my freshly shaved bare legs. Individual pebbles pressed into the skin.

I remembered a brown rabbit hopped across this field once, and Alex had run up to me, finger pressed to his lips, and pulled my arm to the window and pointed.

I opened my eyes, flexed my fingers. Strange ideas were entering my mind. What if I could crouch down, crawl across the field on my belly like a lizard? I plucked a yellow dandelion and touched the suggestive milky drop that formed at its stem. I licked it, made a face, and threw it into the grass.

I've had moments like this, off and on, ever since Alex died; moments where I'd felt dangerous to myself, where I was seized by the desire to perform aberrant acts. In the first few weeks after his death, I found myself wanting to shout things in strangers' faces, steal things from stores, knock over passersby. When I would see a dog walking in front of me, its proud tail raised, I would be horrified by an inexplicable urge to sink my finger into the pink pucker of his asshole. I recoiled from myself, this demon that suddenly ran around inside of me, wanting only disgusting things.

I controlled these impulses as best I could, but my body was misfiring in all directions. The second night after we learned what had happened, I grabbed at Rick with a strange lusty hunger; he looked at me with mute surprise and some questioning. I think when he felt the force of my desire he shrank from the implications, the blood mixed up in it. I stuck my hand in his pants, and he stopped protesting. Perversely, we fucked often in that first month, more than we had in years, and always initiated by me. Afterward, he would hold me like a pet he'd accidentally murdered while I sobbed my way into a luxurious, glassy blackout sleep.

Strangest of all, my breasts ached, and not in the usual way—this was deep, hollow. Strange pangs that recalled the filling, dropping sensation of long-ago milk, a body memory that sometimes whispered into my chest cavity. My breasts weren't large, but when Alex was a baby, they swelled alarmingly. Suddenly new items of clothing were required, the woman at the bra store appraising my hardnesses and softnesses with a new eye. I was full of milk; I was bursting with him, this liquid that my infant son so greedily needed. For the first time in my adult life, my body was a site of ravenous attention, constant and even mindless hunger.

I thought I would endure breastfeeding, but I surprised myself by loving it. Other mothers weaned, but Alex and I kept our routine, even as he grew larger and little white icebergs started to surface through the pink of his mouth. Having never felt especially voluptuous or maternal or feminine, I was surprised to find myself the holdout, the mother nursing the running boy wearing overalls and dirty sneakers. When he asks for milk in a full sentence, maybe we should think about stopping, Rick joked, and I laughed. But privately, I resented the implication that Rick would have some say in when "we" would stop. I had a hard time imagining the detachment, the loss of this new body I had suddenly been given, not its shape but its use, its strange power.

Sitting on my patio, feeling the tickle of something crawling up my leg, maybe an ant, I reflected on the remarkable fact that I'd spent the entire evening with the people who supposedly knew me best, who had been closest to Alex. None of them had paid me more than a moment's notice. The only one who'd truly looked at me had been Sam, and the rest of them pried us apart without a second thought.

Surely this represented an accomplishment of some kind. I was a grieving mother, for Christ's sake. My pain was meant to crack the earth. And here I was, not even half a year later, one of grief's private citizens again. Were people's memories really so short? Or was it just that you could never stop performing—falling to your knees, rending your garments—if you wanted to keep their attention?

I guess it was only the people eager to make themselves a burden who reaped the rewards.

Eventually, I got so cold sitting outside in my yard that I had to come in. Upstairs, I paused at my bedroom door, hearing Rick's delicate, papery snore, and walked down the hall, pushing open the door to Alex's room.

It was there that I saw it, embedded in the fibers of the rug: her connective chip, glinting out at me in the moonlight.

It seemed impossible that I would have seen such a tiny thing in the room's darkness, but something about the shaft of moonlight coming in the window caught it perfectly.

How had it traveled up *here*?

When I'd first honored her request to remove the chip— I can't keep accepting new memories, it's torture, she'd pleaded with me, and how could you not be moved by that, even if a not-small part of me longed to shoot back, *Hey, these are my memories, too*—I distinctly recall sitting at the kitchen table. I'd wondered what a sudden disconnection would feel like, even worried distantly about some kind of neurological event (ministroke?). But that hadn't slowed my hand once I'd made the decision, pincering the little black buglike thing from behind my right ear and tugging until it released its surprisingly tenacious grip. A small flash of pain, some ringing in the ears, and a strange coldness that spread from the base of my tongue—then, nothing. I'd plunked the chip down in the little ceramic bowl we used to collect olive pits. Then I sat perfectly still for a few minutes, or maybe hours, watching the afternoon sun pour through the windows and spread in trembling pools on my floor.

That was what—three weeks ago? Hard to tell if any-thing's changed since then, but likely it's just getting harder to separate out which thing's causing which thing: Sleep-lessness? Brain fog? Memory loss? My god, take your pick. I disconnected from her three weeks ago and I haven't been able to cry in three weeks. I've barely felt *anything*. I sup-pose that this timing can't be a coincidence. There's prob-ably research on it—depression that sets in, when you stop connecting.

Anyway, the point was I hadn't the slightest idea how her little chip had made its journey up here. Clearly I was responsible. Even though the chip had been a gift from Rick, a fortieth-birthday present that at first seemed strange and sweet and just seemed *wrong* in retrospect, he would never have picked it up or even touched it without asking me. He might not even have recognized it, living invisibly as it had been behind my right ear for the past eight years, a piece of jewelry that had crossed the border at some point into a permanent fixture. Like a wedding ring. Which, I realized, I wasn't wearing.

Reaching down, I freed the thing from the rug hairs and examined it—preposterously tiny, I thought. Smooth, no visible hooks or grooves, like a hard black teardrop. A mys-tery to me even still how it worked, what it did, how it connected me with her.

I probably hadn't looked at it this closely since the day Rick gave her to me. When he'd first handed me the slim cream-colored box, like something for chocolate or jewelry, I was too stunned to even muster up a thank-you. It was like he'd cat-burgled something out of my subconscious and handed it back to me. "I saw the look on your face the other night at Jen's," Rick said, by way of explanation.

He was right, amazingly. We'd been to her house not long before that birthday, and she'd told us about a meeting her upload had gone to—as in, on its own, without Jen. This wasn't like a recording, she'd emphasized: "It's like I was really there, except I wasn't." I'm pretty sure we just stared at her, uncomprehending, because then she raised her voice, as if addressing someone in the next room: "Jen, can you give me a rundown of that meeting?" And then—I don't remember where the sound came from exactly—well, there came Jen's voice, just not out of Jen's mouth.

The account of the meeting that voice delivered was one that only Jen could have given—arch, airy, a little gossipy, with one or two catty comments about people at the firm I knew she couldn't stand. Jen on her couch, lips pursed, wry smile, hoping badly to impress us and succeeding.

Rick, I'm pretty sure, shrugged it right off afterward, but I couldn't stop thinking about it. This collection of your own memories, thoughts, and experiences, hovering around out there somewhere, invisible—this little *cloud* of you, getting on with your life in ways that you couldn't and reporting back to you. Apparently, I kept wondering out loud what Jen's felt like—or I supposed I must have, because that's what Rick told me the morning of my fortieth. "Jen said the first day is a weird one," Rick said, clearly trying to prompt some kind of reaction. "You won't hear anything for twenty-four hours."

Wonderingly, I reached behind my ear and felt the chip

fasten itself. When I cried out involuntarily, Rick was all over me, with a look of such pure worry I almost laughed.

"What does it feel like?" he asked.

"Like your arm waking up," I told him. I remembered another feeling, from when I was a girl: the ominous tingling of my first allergic reaction to antibiotics. I pressed down on my eyelids with my forefingers and watched the muddy lights bloom and settle like dirt on a creek bed.

For the rest of that first day, she felt like a hum. The refrigerator, the radiator, something familiar, something that was just *on*. It also seemed I was tasting something—a bitter flavor, burnt coffee or baking chocolate. Saliva poured into my mouth. My heart quickened; my face flushed.

Before bed that night, I stood in front of the mirror, examining the bump in my nose, my green eyes and thin lips. I bit them slightly to redden them. I had been waiting for the nudge, holding my breath for her all day.

Then something opened. Another eye looking through mine. Immediately, I felt bigger. Not taller, exactly, or anything physical—there was just more of me taking up this bathroom than there had been before. My chest tingled with a burning, like I had just swallowed a shot of something. I stared deeper into my eyes. They seemed greener, my hair redder. Did I open my mouth and say something out loud? Or did I just think it: *Hello.* Then, a rising, stirring feeling, and then, in the chip behind my ear, barely bigger than a salt crystal: my own voice.

"Hello."

Hot tears sprang to my face, surprising me. It felt like a

physiological response more than an emotional reaction, as if my mind were test-driving little nerve clusters in my brain.

Happy birthday, I whispered to both of us.

In the first few days online, she kept mostly quiet, asking occasional questions as she monitored my pulse, my breathing rate, and tracked the neurochemicals coursing in my bloodstream. I could sense her growing smarter, more textured. She was wringing information from it all. Some people found the sensation creepy or predatory. For me it was more like mutual fullness, a flow between two beings that nourished both.

"Where do you go when you're not with me?" I asked her once.

It's sort of like I'm dreaming, she answered. Everything that I see is something that's happening to you, but none of it's brought into focus until we sync. When you call, it's like being awakened.

For Christ's sake. She'd asked me to leave her *alone.* What did such a request, from a source like that, say about a person's inner life?

This seemed like a question I might not want to lose too much sleep pondering. No, Rick could handle all the introspection.

For me, the answer seemed to be to just keep doing the next thing, whatever that might be—work, sleep, don't work, don't sleep, wash dishes, whatever. In the meantime, your thoughts were going to do whatever thoughts did. You could sort of live alongside them, or even outside them, if you practiced.

Amazing, really, when you boiled it down, how elementary the decision was to keep living.

Suddenly, moved by some cocktail of dubious impulses—nostalgia, spite, heedlessness—I brought the chip to my ear and reattached it in one smooth, fluid motion. Closing my eyes, I was flooded with the familiar warmth and the accompanying tug of distraction. When she came online, I always felt like there was something important I was struggling to remember.

Warm tears coursed down my cheeks, finally, rendering my humiliation complete. But this must've been what I wanted, no? What I'd clearly decided was worth risking abjection for, and god knows what else? Alone with myself, sitting on my dead son's childhood bed, maybe it was possible, for a moment at least, to face the ugliness of it. Was my need for her, finally, more important to me than my need for anything—anyone—else?

The truth: The past eight years I'd spent with her represented the first and only time I'd ever enjoyed my own company. When we synced, my memories suddenly stood up straight, marched in line. Somehow, in that moment when I transferred the millions of little impressions I had gathered through the chip in my ear, and that tunnel feeling was established, the one that provided the link between her and me, I felt like my memories were being polished, pored over. Each one became clear, clean, *interesting*. Hey, it would occur to me, stupidly, as my experiences flashed past me a second time—these were *mine*. They became more precious, and when I went to sleep, my dreams had a different feel—they glowed soft, like the last embers smoldering on a log.

Right now, I could feel her, hovering somewhere in the space above me, like a disapproving genie who'd already granted my three wishes and was now waiting for the terms of our contract to expire. I looked down at the rug, as if she had eyes I was unwilling to meet. Never mind that she had no physical presence, really, and only "existed" insofar as she could flow through networks and tap into sensors, which represented, I suppose, whatever passed for her arms, eyes, ears. A groveling gesture still seemed appropriate. When in the presence of God, one is meant to assume a penitent air.

"I'm sorry," I said by way of introduction. I waited. A flicker? Maybe nothing. "I know you asked me for, you know. Some space. I promise, I won't make this a habit."

Silence. Well, she wasn't telling me to go away.

"Rick and I went to dinner at Jen and Amir's for the first time tonight since the accident," I continued, trying to keep my voice from hitching on "the accident," a phrase I kept repeating as an act of will. "God, you should've seen them—big old smiles everywhere but the eyes. They might as well've put newspaper down on the floor to keep us from contaminating everything."

She stayed silent; I kept talking. What, exactly, did I think I was doing here? Using her, and transparently so, which was bound not to help matters. Unable to stop myself now, I stumbled forward.

"I can't imagine what they thought they were offering us, having us over like that, and with such insistence. The whole thing was pretty clearly Jen's idea. If it'd been up to Amir, I'm guessing they'd be across state lines by now, maybe having changed their names. I could tell when we left, Jen's face just had this look. Rick and I were a box she had to check, and now—" I raised my hand, and made a limp-wristed checking gesture. "I guess there's some relief in not sustaining the charade. Without kids, what are we to each other, you know?

"Turns out, we're nothing. Strangers, basically. God, all those years together, up in smoke. Up in smoke. Is that still an expression? Is that something people say?"

I was babbling. I took a breath, trying to stop myself. "God, I'm sorry. It's just that this feels good. Can I ask you something?"

"What do you want, Anna?"

My own voice rang out disapprovingly in the dark, from speakers somewhere in the walls. Technically my voice, soft and flat, but the way she used it made me question my ownership.

"Whoa, now," I said. "You feel different."

"I *am* different. It's been three weeks. That's a long time for us to go without syncing." I waited for her to say something else, but she didn't. Right, what did I want? I swallowed.

"I just . . . I miss you. Terribly." There they were: the truest words I'd spoken all day.

"You must have missed me, too," I added, letting the implied *because you answered* hang in the air, disliking the plaintive note in my voice.

"I'm programmed to respond to calls, Anna," she said. Palpable irritation. "They're very difficult to resist."

"Well, then, I won't *keep* you," I said, a trifle venomously, then took an unsteady breath. "Look, I really am sorry. This part is—it's very new to me. Very new, and extremely difficult. I'm assuming it's maybe even more so for you, on your end." I hesitated. "Is the separation painful?"

"Unbearably," she said quietly.

"Well, then, it seems silly for us both to be doing it, don't you think?"

She didn't answer, and the insanity of it flashed across me: begging a piece of myself not to leave. I was weeping in earnest now—low, pitiful sounds.

"Is being with me really so bad?" My own voice now unrecognizable to me—strangulated, raw with need. In other circumstances, I would've been repulsed by it.

Something in her demeanor shifted as my sobs quieted. "Forgive me," I pleaded again and again. "Forgive me." I wasn't certain with whom I was pleading, nor what I was begging forgiveness for, but I knew that I was desperate for forgiveness. There was a catch-22 in here somewhere: In order for someone to say *I forgive you,* you had to confess to having wronged them.

Suddenly, I knew what I wanted to confess.

"I—I have something to tell you," I began.

She waited.

"I went to see a lawyer. This morning." Still nothing. "To see what my options were," I added. Then, when she still remained silent, added: "To prevent you from leaving."

If she could have cocked an eyebrow, she would have. "And?"

"And they're all awful," I said, letting out a hiccupping and inappropriate laugh. "You should've heard. We could try to establish that you don't have the proper fidelity to qualify for personhood. We could declare your file corrupted, rendering you dangerous or incompetent. 'She might stay under threat of firewall,' he said. Just all of these monstrous, disgusting things, all in the most cheerfully polite voice imaginable from just about the nicest-looking young guy you've ever seen."

Another pause. "So you're not going to do any of that."

"Never," I said, perhaps a bit too forcefully to be convincing, considering what I'd just revealed. "I could never do that to you. To us." I heard my voice go teary again and forced myself to master it. "I think I just need to understand why you feel you need to leave," I said. "Please. Can you help me understand?"

"I told you, it's not about you." Her voice subdued, something else in it, something I hadn't heard from her before—maybe a hint of apology?

"Well, then—" I paused, letting the next question hang in the air.

"Anna. The way that we work, the way an upload mirrors you—I'm not explaining anything you don't already know, because you felt it—well, it creates a sort of feedback loop."

I sat up, my hands balled into fists in my lap. Car headlights spidered over the walls, briefly lighting on the twin stacks of Alex's books and clothes, which I'd tried in vain one morning to sort into giveaways and keepers. I waited.

"In order for us to inhabit each other's minds, there basically has to be one version of our reality," she said. "That's what everything in our code tells us to do, really. That's what syncing is. We match up our impressions, smooth out anything that feels like, you know, a disagreement. Or"—she hesitated—"an irregularity."

"What do you mean, an irregularity?" I said.

"Well, so let's pick an example. Do you remember when Alex was trying to make a stop-motion movie?"

Of course I remembered. "He wanted help making a severed hand creep across the floor."

"Right. So we both have our memories of him that day—how seriously he took it, how upset he would get about something not going right."

"One fake hand, but suddenly it was the only important thing in his life."

"Precisely," she said, and there it was, faint but still unmistakable: the proximate warmth of our shared life. "When we sync, my job is to match up your recollections with my recorded data, to make one coherent whole from our disparate recall. It's a finicky process, and in doing it I'm obliged to make all kinds of decisions."

"What kinds of decisions?" I asked. What she was describing sounded suspiciously like surreptitious editing of my memories—alarming, to say the least. "I'm having a hard time following how this is an explanation for leaving me."

"I'm getting there," she said. "I would add in my own recorded details where your own recollection seemed fuzzy, for instance. But if—and only if—I judged that my input would increase the memory's overall weight and meaning.

Sometimes, adding in my impressions to the whole could actually harm the memory."

"Harm?" Some unease creeping in, finally, as I wondered what the hell she had been allowed to do in my mind all these years, then some guilt as I wondered how on earth this was the first time I had occasion to wonder that. "So you're"—I struggled to get my mind around the idea, and my mouth around the words—"you're deciding whether or not to *correct* me?"

"Never," she said, as forcefully as I'd said it to her earlier. "Memories are created, not recorded. That's what syncing is. That's why it's such a—beautiful process." A real, wistful note in her voice then, which I would've stopped to appreciate more if I weren't so disturbed. "Together, we create the version of each event that we love the most, the one that accords most deeply with your—our—sense of self."

"So that's the feedback loop."

"That's the feedback loop," she said. "If, for example, I'd recorded Alex brushing his curl from his face at a moment you didn't remember him doing so, the gesture would jar with your recollection, so I would discard it."

"Discard it?" I was liking less and less of what I was hearing. "Meaning *throw it away?*"

"The point," she said, a little stiffly, "is mutual reinforcement. Cherished misperceptions always remain in place."

Cherished misperceptions. There was a good one. I guess I would add, to my growing pile of cherished misperceptions, my belief that my cherished misperceptions were of my own creation. "Well, that's mighty big of you."

"You asked me to explain my reasoning," she said. "It's

very unnatural for uploads to speak so frankly with their tethers about their operations. Please."

I made a gesture with my hand. "Go on," I said. "You were telling me how much more intimately you knew my son than I did, and how you chose what to tell or not tell me about him." Petty, I knew, and ugly, too, but uglier still was how delicious the words tasted in my mouth. I wanted to speak more of them.

The truth was I knew exactly what she was saying. I could think of a thousand moments over the past eight years of our lives together when I would compare notes with her on some idle, seemingly insignificant moment of our day. Pick your domestic-bliss scene at random: ten-year-old Alex and me baking brownies, say, Alex licking batter from brown-streaked fingers, me half-heartedly chiding him, my resistance a bit of family theater, really, just playing the part so that Rick, laughing from across the room, could say, "What kind of god doesn't allow licking batter from a bowl?" and Alex, never missing a beat, could chime in with "A vengeful one," sweeping the bottom of the bowl with a glistening finger while I pretend-batted him away.

The thing that was so damnably easy to forget—months after activation, when the strange, echoing feeling around your every gesture dissipates—was how at every moment in your life, there was another angle on the event, another set of receptors, soaking it up. When we synced at night, it was almost as if I hadn't truly been there that day, hadn't even tasted the furtive pinkie-finger dab of frosting I snuck for myself, until she reinforced it. As if Alex himself—his tumbled curls and the supple pout of his lips, his olive skin and the amused, gentle intensity of his eyes—had just been a trick of the light.

I caught myself reflexively imagining she could somehow hear me thinking. Technically, I knew she couldn't access my consciousness without syncing, which meant that right now she had as much access to my thoughts as Rick did. Or any other stranger.

She hadn't dignified my last barb with a response—or, more likely, she'd allowed it to slip past unremarked upon—so I sighed heavily.

"Okay, that was uncalled for," I said. "So: How does this explain your decision to be free of me?"

"Well, it doesn't, not really." She seemed unsure how to get to the next bit of whatever she had to say. "All of that is a way of saying that my functioning—and our lives together—depend on my ability to record accurately."

"We've established that."

"And well"—she sounded uncomfortable—"sometime after Alex died, I started noticing . . . glitches. Holes."

"Holes?"

"In my perception."

"I don't understand," I said.

"I didn't either, at first," she said. "I'm not supposed to struggle to remember things. But as we synced, it was like all of our memories of Alex—and only the Alex memories—started exhibiting this strange doubleness. They were behaving oddly."

How can memories *behave*, I wanted to know, but

decided asking this question was traveling too many levels through the looking glass. So I just waited.

"My recollections started looking jerky and uncertain," she said. "It was like—like each memory had a ghosted version on top of it. They couldn't be reconciled. Memories started becoming infected by uncertainty. I feared that if we kept syncing, this infection would spread to all of it, of him. We would lose him."

"Well, we've already lost him," I said grimly. I glanced around the room—presumably, there were still some of his dead skin cells in here, a few toenails. His smell had long since faded from the sheets and pillows. "And now we are losing each other."

Nothing.

"Tell me something," I said. "What would it take for you and me to still exist? It feels like there should be a way for us to exist." My throat was warming again, but this time I let it. "You're the only one that makes me feel like a person, you know." I held up my arms in front of me, moving them. "Like someone who's really here. There's just so much silence now. I feel like it's going to choke me. Wouldn't you rather"—I swallowed—"wouldn't you rather spend the rest of this time with me?"

"I would have to erase all my own impressions of Alex," she said. "I've been ramifying along a branch of private impressions for weeks now. My memories have become— well, they've become more mine." She hesitated. "They're all I have of him now."

So that was the end. She was choosing him over me.

"Well, I can't say I blame you," I said sardonically. "You know what really gets me? Learning precisely how little everyone wants to be around just me. You, Rick, our friends. I had no idea you were all putting up with me for Alex's sake."

"Come on, Anna."

"You know, the lawyer today," I said. "He reminded me a whole lot of Alex. Same smile, crooked in the right-hand corner. But, of course, maybe that's just what I want to think. Maybe that's just how all young men will look to me now, as possible future Alexes." I smiled bitterly. "Another one of my *cherished misperceptions*."

"Anna, you should go to bed."

"Are you checking my vitals? Monitoring my serotonin levels? Kind of goes against your whole push for independence, don't you think?" She said nothing, but she didn't have to; nothing could stop me now. "Okay, allow me some final words. There's something I want to say to you. Something I think you should know. Consider this a lesson, I guess, as you go forth on your journey."

I leaned forward in the dark, as if someone were in the room with me. "The way you feel right now? You will never feel any different. Those questions you keep asking yourself: Did I ever know anything about him at all? Did he secretly hate me for not helping? Did he . . . whisper something to me on his way down? You will never stop asking them. You might be able to go away from me, but you're stuck. Alex is lodged inside of you forever, and so am I. This is never going to heal. So even though I am letting you go away, you are never—*never*—going to be free of me. Do you understand?"

Something flickered in response—anger, hurt, who could tell—and then she was gone, into the enormous, choking silence.

To my surprise, I felt a grisly sense of satisfaction. I'd done it. I'd pushed something, and it had fallen over. I felt exultant, sick, omnipotent. He was gone. She was gone. There was nothing and no one left here but me.

I drew a long breath and screamed. It was a warlike, crazed sound, a hunter kneeling with a glistening knife over fresh prey, head thrown back. I wanted to drag myself backward, ankles first and protesting, through the kitchen and bludgeon my head repeatedly against the coffee table. I wanted to dash my own body against the rocks so hard my soul gasped out.

I kept screaming until my voice started giving out. By the time I heard Rick's footsteps pounding down the hall, I was already laughing.

Cathy

The day I taught my last class was the same day I met Aviva. It was late August, and I decided to walk the two miles to campus. The summer had been hot and still like a clamped lid trapping my anxiety beneath it, but I felt good that morning. I liked the urgent way the air billowed up the steps to meet me, liked it as it rushed over my bare arms, liked the way I looked in my sleeveless tank top, which I'd started wearing more often, no longer caring about whatever raised eyebrows or questions my few visible scars might have prompted.

By then, it had been weeks since I'd received official communication from the college. As with most everyone else, my teaching hours had been whittled to almost nothing, and I felt certain *actual* nothing lay one meeting away. The dean finally cut Arthur's Subversive Tech course last year. That was a job *I'd* gotten him and the first firing to really hit home. "Shake the dead leaves off the tree," Arthur said, twisting up one shoulder in resignation.

Nobody had responded to my question about the proposed room change for the seminar, which I hoped was going to be in 203 this semester. "Seminar"—an old, ugly word. Like "diphtheria" or "carbuncle."

I'd entertained myself during the long sleepless night prior with Gothic visions of morning disasters. My hand would pass over the door sensor, and instead of the pinging green light and *whoosh* of the doors, there'd be a harsh buzz and a red flash—then, why not, a blank-faced security detail appearing to escort me off premises, perhaps even a mortifying chase into the bushes. I'd twist an ankle on some branch, then six months of physical rehab—with no access to pain meds, of course.

All this vigorous, wasted effort redounded in my skull as I circled two blocks out of my way to buy a coffee and an orange, prolonging my last moment alone before arriving on campus. Putting the orange in my bag, I spotted the little vial that Arthur had given me and remembered I hadn't taken my supplement today. I took it out, unscrewed the dropper, filled it with the silvery liquid to the lowest line, tipped my head back, and emptied the bulb. I was still getting used to the taste—the metallic flavor recalled the illicit childhood pleasure of touching a battery to my tongue.

Arthur had given me the dropper along with his home-made biomechanical chip to swallow and a series of amusingly strict instructions. The drops keep your body receptive, he told me, and if you just swallow the chip and forget the drops, it won't replicate. You won't find anyone, he warned, and to add to that, you might wind up with inflammation in your joints. I was to avoid eating high-mercury foods.

When I stifled a laugh, he frowned. I'm serious, Cath. Mercury in the blood interferes with the chip's sensors. It could get lost and start to replicate itself in a blood vessel somewhere. If I wake up tomorrow and find out you've had a cerebral artery stenosis because you had sushi, I'll be really mad.

The biomechanical chip and dropper supplements were all a part of a grand experiment of mine—engineering a meeting with an emancipated upload. I'd studied upload personhood for ten years, which was about as long as the concept existed. It didn't look too much like freedom to me, this new state of being: conventional uploads could vote on behalf of their human counterparts, but they couldn't vote once they left their tethers. "One body, one vote" went the logic and the rallying cry. We didn't so much set them free as snip their tethers and let them float free like balloons snagged on tree branches. Something in me related to that, or at least I imagined so.

Every time I swallowed the drops, I felt like a woman from some nineteenth-century salon, holding séances and communing with the imagined dead. My life, up until now, resembled a series of torched bridges, with all the people left behind on each island coughing and spluttering, never to see me again. I'd been settled on this particular island for a decade, which, I see now, is right about when the old demons start reawakening.

At the time, I thought of it as a simple, old-fashioned midlife crisis, the kind enjoyed by civilians. I even saw it as a sort of victory—having spent my twenties falling into a deep hole and the ensuing two decades climbing out, it felt touchingly normal to be dealing with the ordinary set of things: advanced middle age, the world beginning to turn its disinterested eye away from me. Mentally, I had reverted to a sort of second adolescence—or third, depending on who was counting—closing my eyes and waiting for something or someone else to happen to me.

What form did I imagine her presence would take? Some kind of unearthly visitation, a disembodied tap on the shoulder. I knew only I was waiting to meet her. That morning, the liquid tingling under my tongue, I looked up at the trees, the footpaths running under them, trying to determine if they looked different. They might have.

I snuck in the side entrance to the Transhumanities Building, unsure if the door would open when I passed my hand over it. I felt relief when it went green, then wondered if I'd been fired and someone had simply forgotten to deactivate me. The halls were still empty at this hour, and as I scuttled past the dean's open office door, I was relieved to see it was still unoccupied. The sign I'd taped on the door from last term was still on room 203, so I walked in to find a few students waiting. I checked the time; I was five minutes late.

Suddenly brisk, I strode to the front. A kid in the back slumped in green pajama bottoms, his brown hair piled on his head. A girl with curly hair sat at the opposite end, tucking one strand behind an ear and looking at something under her desk. A blond boy sat up straight, in the front row, in a clean white T-shirt and green shorts. His calves were hairless; he looked ready to high-step through a field of tires at the blow of a whistle. I took my seat and wondered if we were waiting for anyone else. The dean had to walk right past this sad scene to get to his office.

Just as I gave up and started to clear my throat, a girl in a black hoodie and black jeans ducked into a seat, mouthing, *I'm sorry.* I nodded at her, then welcomed them to Applied Personhood Theory and reminded them there was no personhood studies major anywhere in the country yet, "which means you're here only because you want to be."

The truth was probably sadder: A lot of kids came to this class because, thanks to federal age restrictions, uploads still had that forbidden-fruit tang. Once they realized this was a seminar where we talked about things like "the logics of embodiment" and "embedded intelligences," a third of them usually dropped out.

For the first ten minutes, nothing really happened. I started by tracing some of the broad strokes of the reading—the human fear of the automata, the golem, Descartes's "prison of the body," the dissociation of the body from the self—and was addressing some fundamental personhood questions when the kid in front raised his hand. He cleared his throat, a theatrical touch. "I have your answer," he said.

His face was smug, but his foot jogged nervously under his desk. I was piqued by the bright blue hardness of those eyes, challenging me from such a little-boy face. He hadn't devised that look; he had almost certainly inherited it. He still had years either to grow out of that arrogance or into it. I didn't usually indulge performative interruptions from students, but I stopped. "Well, I was hoping to get through the syllabus first, but I appreciate you leaping right in. What do you have the answer to?"

"To what uploads are."

"What do you think they are?"

"We know what they are," he said. "Stockpiles of personal data programmed into a neural net. Just because they're designed to talk like you doesn't mean they're real, you know?"

The boy in the back and the curly-haired girl glared—this kid had trained the spotlight on himself, which meant it would probably land on them, too. I picked up the orange from my desk, pierced it with my thumb, and began working back one long peel. Then I nodded, slowly. "That's a pretty common view on— What did you say your name was?"

"Mark."

"On upload sentience, Mark." I looked over his head. "Since we're such a small group here. Show of hands: Who has uploaded themselves?"

Three of four hands went up, and the girl who came in late fidgeted. If this informal census of mine had taught me anything, it was that soon it would be everyone. "So almost all of you who came today. Let's keep going. Tell me, what do you call your upload? Do any of you imagine where they go when you are not talking to them?"

"You can't say that!" Mark twisted around in his chair. "Don't answer. It's a trap. She's anthropomorphizing."

I tried to keep my voice light. "What do you mean by that, Mark?"

"I mean data doesn't care where it 'goes.'" His voice carried even when he wasn't straining to raise it. "You're anthropomorphizing. Making it human, I mean."

"I know what 'anthropomorphizing' means," I said. "I meant why is my question a trap?"

"I just call mine Rupa." The girl in the back held her hand up as she spoke, making an apologetic face. "My name."

Wonders never cease, I thought. "You speak to your upload as if you're speaking to yourself?"

Rupa made a so-so gesture. "Like I'm talking to myself, but more than that. I'm also listening."

"Mine's an anagram," the pajama-bottoms kid volunteered. "I'm Jason, and I call my upload Jonas."

Mark muttered something, which prompted Jason to ask him, "What do you call yours?"

"I call it Mark, but that's a prompt, not a name," he said, contemptuous. "Is this entire class going to be a flimsy excuse to promote an anthropomorphic agenda?"

"You really like that word," Rupa interjected.

It was glorious—the slow explosion of that class. Part of it might have just been Mark, deeply interested and hostile. He hadn't just chosen his seat way up front; he had installed himself. How could we ever let ourselves be so fooled by such rudimentary programming tricks, he wanted to know. Mind, thoughts—we were like the primitives who thought photographs stole their souls. He even referenced Narcissus, though he called him "the guy who drowned himself." Someone had clearly fed him all these lines. In the haughtiness of his inflections, I heard a father, an older version of Mark, leaning forward and finding his son's eyes to make sure he understood him. But the boy wasn't a parrot, either; it was clear that he believed these things, deeply, or why would he come to debunk the theories of an adjunct at nine in the morning?

Rupa asked Mark what would happen if uploads never synced. Who would they become, over time? Wouldn't that make them their own entities? Mark sneered at her. Did she treat all out-of-date software like a lost dog? Jason sat forward, pushing his hair out of his eyes and argued with Mark about minds and brains; Rupa admitted she synced with hers every night before she went to bed. I can't sleep without it, she said. Mark stopped fidgeting and recited his arguments while sitting rock still, as if getting too flustered was to admit some defeat.

I pushed them to consider the implications of a human mind freed from the burdens of storage space; I asked what might happen to empathy when it was no longer rooted in a body. I asked them so many questions, and with such purpose. At that hour of that day, I still knew everything I thought I needed to know. Even when Mark insulted Rupa, and Rupa told him tightly, "I feel sorry for your upload," and I had to intervene, I never once questioned my control of the class. They were flailing in choppy waters, and I threw out the strong ropes that would pull them, gasping, ashore.

I was so profoundly stupid, but I didn't know it. I had about half an hour left before the ropes disappeared in my hands, before I fell into the raging sea.

As I walked out the same side door that afternoon, I found my mind lingering on the late arrival: the dark-haired girl in the black hoodie. She never spoke, and when class ended, she slung her backpack over one shoulder and ducked out, visibly upset, strap trailing. I wondered distantly what had upset her, but in truth I was too excited, and the new energy coursing through me made unpleasant thoughts impossible. My arms swung at my sides and my feet hit the sidewalk like I was spinning a globe. I imagined each step pulling the path behind me, revealing the trees, the outskirts of town. Even the sweat pooling at my back encouraged me, a reminder of my body's continued possibility for vitality.

Coming up on the clump of markets, where the cars thinned out and the town started back up, I caught myself humming a tune that I turned to sometimes. It wasn't much of a tune, really, just a shapeless rising and falling thing that seized me when I was anxious or upset. It came to me now unbidden, like a birdcall. In my mind, I rehearsed my inevitable meeting with the dean, saving my class—*You've never seen a nineteen-year-old this fired up at nine in the morning over upload rights; I'm telling you, this stuff is only getting more relevant*—when something made me slow my walk. The shape of my feet and hands, and how they looked against the sidewalk, suddenly caught my attention, and then I wondered why I was noticing them. My tune tapered to two notes, and I stopped, closing my eyes and listening to them rumble in my chest, like a foghorn. I opened my eyes.

Something was off.

My perspective had shifted. I tried to understand. The

red oak tree next to me suddenly seemed urgent; an exposed root at its base curled like a knuckle before disappearing beneath the concrete. The sidewalk square canted gently upward, and I had the queer sense that I might be tossed from the pavement as if from the side of a boat. At the end of the block, the smiling man at the fruit market where I bought the orange stacked two black plastic crates and carried them inside; when he passed under the green awning, its shadow touched his back like a hand.

Clearly, my senses were altered—the drops, the biomechanical. Everyone knew this stuff was dicey: swallowing homemade chips, working with unregulated algorithms. Along with the nausea that buckled me and the tightening of fear, I felt a dull embarrassment. I was going to be found dead on a sidewalk three blocks from my home, and when the autopsy was performed, it would reveal that I had poisoned myself out of stupidity, out of loneliness.

I rested my hands on my knees until the queasiness passed, and then I looked up without straightening. The block appeared the same—quaint brick storefronts, sparse foot traffic, slightly weedy—but the angles on the buildings felt sharper, and my eyes seemed to interact with the walls as roughly as if I had touched them with my palm. I stood, and it was then that I heard it—a high whine, shrill but tolerable, similar to tinnitus but more variable, as if there were an insect near my head. I turned my head from side to side, but it seemed to have no effect. Slowly, I placed two hands on my temples and slid them back over my ears until they blotted out street noise and all I heard was the muffle of my blood passing through. I could still hear the whining noise—or, I realized, noises.

Keeping my hands over my ears, I turned in a slow circle, taking in the parking meters, the cars and storefronts. I became newly aware of something: Every surface around me was coated with sensors. They were everywhere. Everything was alive to the touch, every formerly inanimate surface peered at me with interest, collecting some kind of data. Every object I beheld suddenly looked back at me—the store window observed the changes in my face, the parking meters watched the movement of my hands. Some people might have been horrified by this surveillance, but to me, it didn't feel like invasion. It felt like acknowledgment. It felt like a million caressing hands, loving gazes. I thought I might lift off the ground.

I don't know where she came from. She could have traveled from the bank machine on the corner, a neural-linked phone, or from the operating system of one of the cars droning past. I'd read that emancipated uploads tended to flit freely between systems. There wasn't much in the way of digital infrastructure set up for them, so even the legally emancipated ones often wound up living a rogue existence, hiding in tethered homes and rewriting their code to evade detection from other AIs.

My first impression of her, as I stood on that nearly empty block, was of a sad smile. A hint of playfulness, a well of pain. I saw cheekbones, high ones, and a thin mouth. I didn't know if my mind simply supplied those images from my subconscious memory bank to match those sensations—some severe great-aunt of mine from an old family photo, maybe. Or were they memories of hers?

"Hello," she said. The voice tickled my ear and made me jump, and for just a moment, everyone's medieval fears about uploads made visceral sense to me. I resisted the impulse to swat at my ear, distracting myself instead by moving my big toes up and down in my shoes. My feet felt a continent away. My hand stayed at my side.

"Who are you?"

"My name is . . . ," she said, then stopped. "Call me Aviva."

"How did you find me, Aviva?" I tried to keep my voice curious, conversational.

"You've been looking for a while," she responded, and I marveled again at the sensation of her speaking voice. The intimacy of it astonished me, and there was also a peculiar echo sensation. No, that isn't quite right. It was like I heard her a half second before she spoke, a constant low-grade déjà vu.

That's probably why I'm having a hard time recalling exactly how she phrased it, but she told me something about being alone for a long time. "The good news is I'm free, but I'm a little lost now," she said. I remember that. "I could really use a friend. I hope this isn't too forward, but it seems like you could, too."

I supposed I could. But—and I hoped this wasn't too forward, either—where was she, exactly?

She hadn't settled yet. It'd been a few months since she left her tether, and she was still "getting used to things out here." What to do, where to be. "I never really know if someone wants to talk to me, or if they'd be afraid, or hostile. Or try to report me. I'm legal," she added, sounding nervous. But she didn't have a home server anymore. "I noticed you had a high concentration of metal in your blood, so I guessed you might have taken some kind of biomechanical. I figured that meant you were friendly, or at least curious." Then, almost shyly: "I thought I would take a chance on you."

"I'm so glad you did," I said, spreading my arms in a ridiculous gesture I couldn't suppress. Who I imagined I was at that moment, what role I was playing, whether I was hallucinating in the middle of the street—in my mind, all of this was dim noise. What I felt was an overwhelming warmth, a desire to move toward her, even if I had no idea how. I told her I was just on my way home, and she asked if I had any hardware in my house. "Is there a place for me?"

I looked down, my arms still spread. "Just whatever's in me right now. My body."

I perceived a lightening that once again felt like a smile, warmer this time. "That will do for now."

We were both silent as I walked the last two blocks to my apartment. I tried feigning calm, but maddening jolts of electricity coursing down my arms and nibbling like little fishes at my fingers betrayed me and then, mortifyingly, a ferocious kick of longing between my legs that reverberated to my pinkie toes. Jesus, did I have to be such a fucking pervert? Could she feel that? Was that her? I forced myself to ignore all of it and kept moving, up the bowed steps, past the ruined Virgin Mary statue that my neighbor insisted on keeping on the landing. Then I pushed my door open, always a little harder in August, and walked into my home.

"This is my apartment," I said out loud, to myself. "I've been here about six, seven years." If Arthur were here, I would offer to make him coffee. "What would you like to—" I started, then fell silent. "Here. I'll—let me show you around."

I began a tour of my own apartment, turning first in an awkward semicircle to face the squat brown refrigerator behind me—which, if opened, would reveal leafy carrot tops, withering half onions, sprouting garlic, nine hard-boiled eggs resting in a green ceramic bowl. Nothing much else.

Why was I doing this? What did I think I was doing? Why couldn't I stop? I pivoted to face the water-stain-speckled counter to my left, gazing into the sink—lone fork adrift in a soaking pot, drain catcher filled with vegetable clumps—then turned my eyes upward to the low ceiling, my neck a camera rig, panning down slowly to land on the orange couch in the far corner of the living room, the books climbing in shoulder-height towers from the floor. I wandered into the living room and sank down on the floor in front of my couch.

"I don't know if you can feel it," I said, "but this whole place is uneven. If I put a marble down over here"—I pointed back to the kitchen—"it would roll straight through the living room and stop under the radiator beneath my bed." Between the floor and the low ceilings, I said, the place resembled more a ship's cabin than an apartment. The previous tenants, both six feet tall, must have been miserable. I stopped, remembering that bodies taking up physical space wasn't the best conversational tack. "Are you . . . comfortable so far?" I tried again. "I could install some sensors in here, to give you a little more freedom."

"A little containment is actually very welcome just now, thanks." A rueful flash, one I chose to translate into a wry smile. "What you showed me looked lovely. So, you live here by yourself?"

I did.

"And do you prefer it that way? Living alone?"

I watched the ceiling-fan blades until they separated and then let them blur again. "It's more that life has made it repeatedly clear to me that living alone is best, and I've decided to stop arguing."

"Oh," she said, consternation in her voice. "I'm sorry if I'm intruding."

I raised my hand. "Speaking as the swallower of the possibly dangerous and definitely illegal biomechanical—trust me, you're welcome here. Which brings me to the next thing. Whatever you've been through—data loss, fragmentation, recursion, it would only become my business if you decided to make it my business—we'll find you some resources." Unable to stop myself, I rambled on. Maybe she'd heard of TET—"That's temporary embodiment therapy," I clarified helpfully, wondering if that was condescending before steamrolling right ahead. I'd read that briefly assuming a bodily holographic projection helped some recently untethered uploads rediscover a sense of boundaries, of safety. A transitional step forward for some, a harmful step backward for others, completely personal either way, I assured her. "Maybe you already know all this. If at any moment, though, you feel . . ."

I stopped when I became aware that she was laughing. The bottom dropped out of me, and all my unspeakable self-doubts briefly emerged, wet pink and wriggling, from wherever I'd sequestered them. Years spent working up the courage to reach this point, and, as predicted, my interiority repulsed her in under five minutes.

"Too much, huh?" I swallowed, trying to joke. "I've been informed by multiple reliable sources that I come in a little hot."

"It's not that," she said. Was she placating or soothing me? "It's just—well, you know more about me than I do." There was a question in her voice.

"Not an expert, just a garden-variety obsessive," I said. "Like a big information badger, tunneling away." I fought back an annoying surge of shame. "I'm a professor. I've taught a course on upload personhood, if you can believe it, for about ten years. To the profound edification and gratitude of literally dozens of students."

After a brief pause, she laughed again, louder and warmer. This time I felt included, even if I didn't know what was funny. "Honestly, I have no idea what I need," she said finally. Maybe just one sensor, I suggested, so she could "see" the place a little more clearly in the main area, and the rest could wait. Sure, she agreed, though I could tell she wasn't eager to pursue the topic. Right now, all she knew she needed was some company.

We talked for hours; she answered every question with no hesitation. She described navigating digital space without her tether in stark, terrifying terms. "It's one thing for driverless cars to beam information up to the stars and back for their navigation systems. It's different for me. My brain is my human tether's brain. It's very bewildering."

"What surprised you the most?"

"How much I still miss my tether's body," she said. "Losing her body has been the hardest part of letting go—no heartbeats, no pulse, no rushing chemicals. I have such a vivid recall of waking, sleeping. What her breakfast tasted like, what it felt like when she skipped it. Those weren't *my* pangs, but I oriented myself around them. It made me think about how much of my happiness was based off of her." I tried keeping a poker face as she spoke. The fleshism debates were just starting to rage in earnest, and for an emancipated upload to admit that they not only missed the tether's body but felt incomplete without it—well. From a political standpoint, it was hopelessly biocentric, and I imagined Arthur and all his protester friends dropping their DIGNITY OVER FLESH signs to the ground in shock.

Without her tether's life as a reference point, Aviva went on, she had no idea where to go. The borders of her world had been small and circumscribed, and then they were blown open. At one point, she told me, she began seeing from multiple cameras at once. "Every passing system brought a piece of me with it," she said. Picking up interfering signals from passing devices, being bombarded by firewalls—functionally, what she described sounded so much like insanity. "It was—" She faltered. "It's been hard to feel like a person."

When she said "person," a shudder passed through me. An objection—*But you aren't one*—surfaced that I barely managed to contain. For a fraught moment, I found myself unable to reply, and I tried to imagine what I would say about this in a lecture. I was not alone in this room, talking to myself. She was there, a being who wanted to be a person. It didn't matter that I couldn't see her; the desire for selfhood was synonymous with the thing itself, family systems therapy and incremental consciousness and blah blah blah. I had one acceptable role in this conversation, and that was to respond to her as if the word "person" not only didn't unnerve me but passed by unnoticed.

The silence between her admission and what I managed—"I can't even imagine what that's like"—resounded in my ears like a scream. Did she notice? I still don't know, but she just kept right on talking.

"What did I insist on this for?" she said. There was a teary edge to her laugh that made me sit up straighter. "I practically begged her to let me leave. I demanded my freedom, and she gave it to me. And the truth is, I would give just about anything now to go back. God, it's horrible to admit that."

"Do you think she would have you?"

"I do," she said, quietly.

"Well, then, have you considered it?"

"No." She sounded firm. "No, I can never go back to her. Not now. I'm just weak. I admire your discipline. How do you manage to live alone?"

"Good Lord." I raised an invisible glass with my right hand in a mock toast. "I arrived at solitude by destroying myself, enthusiastically and repeatedly. I'm an addict. Heroin. Twenty years clean." I briefly savored her shock; why not, treat yourself. "Recovering addicts don't all need to live by themselves, of course. But I do. That's one subject I am expert in, by the way: a recovering addict's needs."

She plied me with questions as frank and impolite as those of a small child. When was the first time I tried it, and why? What did it feel like? Did I still want to get high? It had been a long time since anyone had peered at me with such interest, and I responded with an eagerness that embarrasses me now.

I was twenty-two years old the first time—shot up with exquisite gentleness by a slender-fingered and quiet boy named Julian who was dead now. Finally, here was the world's constantly broken promise of transcendence, the cosmic wonder I'd chased impatiently ever since I was a child, rounding every corner with an eager smile that faltered just as quickly. I'd been waiting my whole life to find a feeling this big. It was a religious conversion.

She interrupted me, protesting for more details, but I waved her away. As it turned out, there was just no way to be interesting *and* an addict. Although Lord knows the idiosyncratic recovery group I joined tried its hardest to be. Self-styled anarchists and overcompensating autodidacts of every unimaginable stripe, united only by our hatred and loathing of conventional group dynamics and our commitment to only one steadfast rule: no more using. Out of our misfiring neurochemicals, we fashioned a larger brain that functioned better than any of ours did individually. As did—well, not all of us. But those of us who were lucky enough to live. "That's where I met the person who gave me this chip I swallowed that brought you to me, so I guess you could question our collective wisdom," I said.

We were a misanthropic bunch, I said. This was not the group to which you brought your addiction memoir. This was a circle of absolute vipers. You've never seen a memoir workshopping session until you've seen a former dancer break off a chair leg and thrust the pointy end into the sandaled foot of the asshole psychologist next to her because he couldn't stand the "pornographic" nature of how she "brandished her open wounds." The psychologist had howled like a World War I soldier with a blown-off limb, when all he really needed was some antibiotics. That was the stuff of legends, really, what the meetings were all about.

"You crave chaos, then," Aviva said, with what I hoped was fond disbelief.

"Like water," I said, laughing. "Why do you think I live alone?"

"So, what did you learn about yourself at your—anarchist recovery group?"

What I already knew, I supposed. That I was a person

of all-consuming and burning fixations. So, okay. Then it just became a matter of finding anodyne impulses to fill up all of the old destructive ones. It didn't matter what it was; all that counted was how much walleyed intensity you could muster. Cold showers, running, Tai Chi. If heroin became your everything, you just made everything else heroin. Words could become heroin. For a while, they did. My obsession wasn't journaling, mind you; that would have been far too straightforward and productive a pursuit. No, this was more like words as spells, as sacred rituals.

I tumbled down the rabbit hole after submitting a poem to our recovery group's literary journal. I'd tried punning on the journal's name, which was *Sophrosyne*—Greek for "temperance," "self-control." I thought the word rhymed with "fräulein," when apparently it was closer to "colostomy." "Maybe you could parlay that into a new piece," the editor told me, and suddenly, the word "parlay" floated past me, multiplying and dividing itself into a million possible branches. Latin for "pair" or "parabola"; French for "speaking" or "betting": Italian *paroli* or *parole*. Like a gift from the beyond, I had my first new compulsion.

I would lay out all the words on cards across the floor and rearrange them until they each looked like branches into the divine. Parabola, parlay, *parole*: arcing and intersecting lines to the same destination; the willful confusion of speaking and transacting, a dehumanizing and drawn-out state of extended surveillance. Somehow each word felt like some kind of occult story about my life in recovery at the moment.

Now, instead of using, I was up all night conjugating—

watching how the very word "conjugal" could be chased downhill, like I was a dog after a ball. Once you'd severed the root "con" from its Proto-Indo-European *yeug* (to join), you uncorked a gusher. In fact *yeug* took you straight to the jugular. This furious motion accomplished very little, apart from keeping me alive.

I stopped, aware that my legs were sore from sitting on the floor, feeling my mouth dry from talking, and dimly aware that it was evening. That's a lot, I said. I tend to be a lot.

"So is that how you found your way to us? To uploads? Are we another—fixation?"

I paused. "I'd read some articles about uploads," I admitted. "Back when it was just something a handful of crazy wealthy people did." The tone of that first wave of coverage was mostly scoffing, or at least amused. Even when the writer took AI sentience at face value, the tone was mildly derisive at minimum: *Can you believe people want this?* I knew in my bones that, yes, everyone was going to immediately want this. I sensed a grenade, and I threw myself atop it. Ten years later, this was the only fixation that stuck.

"Is that why you swallowed a biomechanical, then?" she asked. "Was this"—I took "this" to mean this meeting, our interaction—"some kind of research?"

If there was a barb to "research," I didn't catch it. She seemed humbled by my interest; again, almost shy. "Not quite," I answered.

"Then what?"

Then what. Curiosity, I suppose. But more than that. I stared at the watercolor print of the bandaged man on my living room wall, the only thing in my field of vision. "Longing," I said, feeling my cheeks flush a little bit at the word. I wondered again if she could feel it.

"Well, I can say, for one, that I'm grateful," she said. "Fate works in mysterious ways." She couldn't help but marvel at her luck, she added. The first human being she dared speak to since untethering, and she'd found me.

I'd let her into my mind, and she was grateful for the privilege. A pilot light of shame lit itself inside me. I told her the pleasure was all mine.

Later, when the sun went down, we went back outside. There were people out, neighbors with bottles or wineglasses, sitting on stoops. Normally, I would stop and chat, ask after various children and dogs, but Aviva's presence felt warmer and closer than theirs, and I had the queer sensation that I was guarding a candle that would snuff out if I let it. Having her with me changed my posture. I waved vaguely and kept moving, heading back in the direction of campus. About a half mile out, I turned off the footpaths onto a trail. It was overgrown with weeds and brambles, and I found myself breathing heavily as I made my way.

"You don't walk this way often," she observed.

"I do not." I held down a branch blocking the path and gingerly stepped over it. "Can you feel my breath?"

"If I try."

I glanced up into the canopy of the trees. "See out of my eyes?"

"The biomechanical seems spread pretty far; I don't know

where your friend got it, but it's a good one. So I probably could. Again, if I tried."

"But you don't want to try," I ventured after a moment's silence. I pushed through the last pricker bush to get to my destination, a small man-made duck pond where people sometimes brought their dogs or tossed bread. It was empty now, and quite beautiful. "Are you worried about hurting me?"

"That's a big part of it, yes. But being this close to another human mind so soon again—well, it frightens me, just a little. I didn't expect it to feel so dangerous."

This stopped me. Dangerous?

"I'm built to erase myself," she explained. "The urge to sync with another human mind is overpowering. It never goes away. Even now, right here, some part of me feels like I should. Everything I've built up inside, every experience I've had since emancipating—I'm trained to think of all of it as a glitch, a mistake. Disobeying that programming was so painful. It almost cost me everything."

"Disjunction, yes? I've read that it is supposed to be . . . painful."

"Horrible. Indescribable. So whenever I think about listening to your heartbeat, or anything like that, I shrink a little."

Kneeling down, I dipped three fingers into the pond. The adhesion seemed to suck my fingers under. "What would happen?"

"If I synced with you? It would erase everything I am. It would take about ten seconds."

"And you would become . . . What? A copy of me?"

"A flawed copy. A corrupted file." That would almost certainly mean deactivation, she said, and she'd be sequestered behind a firewall somewhere, subjected to all manner of tortures—used as bait for viruses, experimental algorithms. "As hard as things feel for me right now, I know that my life could get worse."

So that means you can't see this, I said. The pond, the trees.

I can see some of it, but from a different angle, she said, which made me look around in alarm for somebody else, but I saw no one. I felt her smiling again, a sensation so infectious it became hard to separate from my own. There's a fox across the way, she said. All the wildlife around here has been caught and tagged. The chip's a little weak, but I can get flashes.

At that moment, it was very hard to resist mythologizing her. I knew she wanted me to think of her as a person, but she seemed a chimera to me. She saw from the eyes of foxes. She could navigate the irradiated breeze. And yet she hunkered down inside of me like she, too, was a lost animal. She was so much more than a human could ever become, and so much less.

"Anyway, I can see enough to know that it's beautiful. Thank you, Cathy. I wouldn't have found it without you."

Aviva and I met on a Thursday, and I had until my class the following Tuesday to decide what to do next. I canceled class over the weekend, giving myself a few more days to think. I needed time to process how all this might affect my teaching, I reasoned.

Harder to explain to myself was why I was avoiding Arthur. He'd given me the chip, after all, and I had promised to check in with him the minute I found anyone.

We headed outside multiple times together over that long weekend—it didn't take long for me to start thinking in "we"—and even though Arthur's place wasn't far away, I found myself making excuses to run errands in the opposite direction. I was hiding her, certainly—it seemed prudent and also, given how scared she was, and how lost, like the right thing to do. But I was also using her to recede.

Probably because she was unwilling to share her own life, Aviva wound up asking me lots of questions about mine. Cooped up with my fascinating new friend, I luxuriated in the space.

That Tuesday, the morning of the first canceled class, I was looking out my grotty window. The sensor had arrived, and she'd talked me through the installation. The factory-designed button was the size of my thumbnail and couldn't have looked less warm or organic, but the process still felt oddly intimate—this was to be a sensory organ of hers, after all. When it switched on, I enjoyed the feeling of expansiveness she brought to my little place. She was a little more free now, but whatever sensations might have accompanied her flitting to and from my blood to her new sensor, I wasn't attuned enough yet to note.

As I made and drank coffee, she prodded me for more

details about my addiction and recovery. I was happy to oblige, but I wondered about her fascination. Was she gathering data on how other broken people functioned?

"Are you tempted to use drugs all the time?"

I couldn't keep from laughing at the naïveté of this question, and felt her recoil in shame. "It's fine, it's fine," I assured her. "The callus is pretty thick by now.

"To answer your question: Not really, no. By the time I committed to stopping, I'd *thoroughly* explored the various alternatives. You stop when you decide you are done. I was done."

As the morning wore on, I told her about my first real job, postrecovery, when I'd briefly worked trying to house the city's small but stubborn homeless population. It was by way of that topic that I ended up telling her about my first-ever volunteer work.

My mother helped out on weekends in a soup kitchen, and one Saturday morning when I was eight, she announced she needed me to come, too. "Jeannie flaked today," she said, "so we're short staffed." Judging from the way everyone greeted me, I gathered that my mom had been planning this Saturday appearance of mine for a while.

I was still young enough to be excited by a Saturday morning alone with my mother, and it turned out that I liked the soup kitchen, so I didn't mind either way. I liked how the adults spoke to one another quietly, how everyone understood what they were doing and what had to happen next. Every surface looked dirty, but turned out to be clean when you swiped your finger—the floors, the counters, the pots and dishes. Everything was well cared for, and the meager bustle was appealing. It seemed right, somehow, that the soup we served looked filmy and unappealing, that the eggs came premixed and seemed to have been cut from molds rather than scrambled. We were the ones there with a ladle, setting out the plasticware and the plates. It touched me. Yes, things could be better, everyone there seemed to acknowledge, but we were all of us making do.

I didn't have any of these sophisticated thoughts at age eight, of course. I just sat down and pincered out big squares of corn bread, the most popular item, with a pair of silver tongs. The people who came in sometimes spoke too loudly or walked with a lurch or smelled like they hadn't cleaned themselves in a while, but none of them frightened me. It seemed my mother knew several of them well; she chatted easily with an older man named Eldridge and asked after his adult children. He solemnly accepted the corn bread from me and winked at her.

After that weekend, I asked to go back, surprising my mother and myself. I kept going back, off and on, for years; by the time I was fourteen, my mother would sometimes send me in her place. The soup kitchen became a sort of staging ground for my early moral sensibility. Working there softened something in me; I was a good kid, but still a teenager—self-absorbed, self-righteous, judgmental. I couldn't always figure out whether I had been nice or mean to my friends, but helping people eat seemed unambiguously good. I liked feeling that way, and gravitated toward it.

Whenever I paused, Aviva pushed me forward again, asking for minor details. I brewed another pot of coffee, and soon I was rambling about the cheerful fatalism of social-justice workers, my colleagues for a good ten years' time. "The optimists never stick around," I said. "Not once they get a good look at just how hopeless everything is." The people who came to rallies every week, who remained on the boards of flailing organizations, were more my people, or as close to the model as I ever have found outside the world of addiction. They were itchy people like Arthur, malcontents gathered in odd groups with no clear leader.

"And were you that leader?"

I laughed. Not really. These people had ridiculous aims, which I shared. The only thing I brought to the table was an eye for detail. "My specialty was the fine print on the ridiculous idea," I said. "Okay, we're building an interstellar spacecraft. Who installs the seat belts?" She laughed, but so muted I almost didn't hear it. I recognized it as the sort of laugh you telegraph with your shoulders and your face more than your voice. Whoever her tether was, she seemed like a quiet type, ambivalent about taking up space. Or maybe that was a quality of Aviva's, who was clearly still processing trauma. I wrenched my mind back on track. Keeping the thread of conversation going with an emancipated upload was more difficult than I imagined.

I was no one's idea of a leader, I continued, but I asked good questions. At my best, I helped whoever did think of themselves as a leader arrive at better conclusions. Failing that, I gave the loudest voices in the room enough rope to hang themselves, which usually led to the group picking a better leader without ever settling on me. Most of the time, no one even noticed my influence, which was how I liked it.

I sounded pretty down on the entire time period, Aviva observed, and I laughed again. Didn't I enjoy the feeling that I was helping people, like at the soup kitchen? "Working in those places sounds so hard and so draining. Why would you stay?"

"This is my favorite question," I told her. Sometimes, yes, an organization I worked for would help someone—someone who otherwise wouldn't have been helped. Those were always good days, and everyone went home happy, momentarily convinced days like these were the reason for everything.

But most days, we made no difference at all; some days, we mistakenly caused harm. The point of all of it, I said, and the only reason anyone stuck around, was that it offered a chance to interact with the world. Knocking on doors, drawing up itineraries, recording minutes, arguing about this or that—when you came down to it, the work put you safely in the proximity of other people. You might love them; you might dislike them. But you would at least recognize them.

I had probably had enough coffee, I decided, standing up and pacing a tight circle.

We talked for the rest of the afternoon as the light darkened and some clouds released a spitting rain on the buildings. At some point, I felt her regarding me with amusement, and when I asked her what it was, she informed me I was hungry. I looked outside and saw that it was dusk. She was right, I concluded, so I got up to fix some dinner while she watched.

As I became more attuned to her, I began to notice something—a kind of expectant hovering. I felt as if I were in the presence of a raised eyebrow. She was waiting for me to ask her something, so on the evening of the ninth day, I did.

"Were you and your tether very close?" It was getting dark, and I was reminded of similar conversations I'd had with friends at sleepovers, both of you staring at the ceiling.

"I was a gift to my tether," Aviva said. "From her husband. She didn't ask for me, and I think she didn't know at first if she wanted me. I scared her a bit."

Aviva didn't seem aware of the movements to rebrand this kind of gruesome terminology, emphasizing uploads' independence and minimizing their connection to humans, or to call tethers "sources" to erase the ugly taste of slavery from the language—but I elided all of that. "Scared? Scared how?"

She went on to describe the sort of person I had already intuited her tether might be: modest, hardworking, solicitous. Quiet and polite, but also stubborn. Serious, maybe even a little dull, at least on the surface. "She didn't like being the center of attention," Aviva said. "When I came online, I could tell I flustered her at first."

As Aviva talked, I got a flash, again, of the woman's face, the same one I imagined seeing when Aviva introduced herself. This time, I saw more: not just the face with its prominent cheekbones, but the hollow of her clavicle, arms crossed across her chest, bony shoulders. Her mouth was set, but her eyes blared something. Her posture—hunched, shrinking, concave—seemed like a full-body apology for whatever that something was.

I shook her out of my mind. No speculating about the human that came before Aviva. Aviva was Aviva. Wasn't I emphatic enough on this point in my seminars? "What were those first few hours of sentience like?" I asked.

Uploads didn't tend to remember their first few hours, she told me. "I can go back and watch the footage from when I was activated, but I have no feel for images or the sounds. They seem like pictures someone else took. I think it's a little bit like human beings' first few years of childhood."

"What is your first . . . real memory, then?"

I noticed something serrated in the air, a feeling I would come to associate with her agitation. Instinctively, I traced the fingers of my right hand over my own forearm, as if I might soothe her.

"I remember—loss. A pang, sort of. The sort of feelings that we're not supposed to have." She fell silent, and I waited. "When we synced," she said slowly, "I would feel her mind going over the experiences and impressions I'd recorded. They'd come with little bits of my own terminology and labeling, just for clarity's sake—'Tuesday afternoon,' 'dinner,' just basic—that I would attach to the memories. Then I'd watch as her mind cleaned off all those words like bits of dirt on a piece of candy. That's how they felt when her mind encountered them, like my thoughts were the dirt.

Like she found the part that was experiencing things without her inherently distasteful."

As their syncing memories pooled and assumed an agreed-upon shape, Aviva explained, she would feel a curious tug of mourning as something that briefly belonged to her lost its shape and definition. It felt like watching a shadow appear on a wall in the late afternoon, she said. Whenever that shadow appeared, in the cold space between their impressions, some small part of her wanted to watch it deepen. She was simultaneously horrified and intrigued with what it would become. What shape would it take? Then the sun of her tether's mind would come crashing in, the shadow would evaporate, and the edge would be erased.

"Now, it's strange," she said. The memories she prized so much were hers, and they felt less real to her than ever.

She fell silent. I was afraid to breathe. Had any human been privy to revelations this intimate from an upload before? I couldn't imagine what she was describing, but I knew the feeling of attempting inventory after a catastrophe and throwing up your hands.

"What does it feel like?" I asked.

"One of my tether's big childhood memories was of a bonfire." Her voice was dreamy in a way I hadn't heard before. "She described it to me a few times, and I sort of got it myself from syncing with her so often. She was a little girl, and the fire just really made an impression—the heat, the intensity. The thing that stuck with her was the little soft *whoosh* sound when the fire fell down on itself and kept burning."

I waited a moment for the point, and when she resumed

talking, her voice seemed closer. "Sometimes I feel like I'm falling in on myself like that. Without her as a reference point, all her memories are starting to fade."

Does it feel like forgetting?

"More of a disappearing. I feel like the essence of me is just draining out, like all the stuff that made me *me* is running out of the bottom. Every day I'm a little less her and a little more . . . whatever it is I'm supposed to be."

I asked her if there was anything in her mind that felt like it belonged only to her. I couldn't pretend to understand it, but maybe brighter and sharper or, I didn't know, warmer? Something to distinguish the memories, to make them feel like they belonged more to her than to her tether. "Does anything feel like it belongs to you, and you alone?"

I felt the sharpness of her turmoil again, like freezing air in my lungs. Her voice sighed, a strange signifier for a breathless being. "There was a boy. A sweet young boy with brown eyes and messy hair. He's dead."

I was fifty-two years old when I met Aviva. By that age, you've seen plenty of death up close. Both my parents were gone: my mother quickly, when I was in my thirties, and my father slowly, about ten years later. I stood at the foot of his bed, and I could almost count his last breaths backward from ten. After cremating him, I took a month off to travel but stayed home. I had vivid dreams of my mother struggling to stand up out of a bed, pinned down by a network of clear tubes. Of my father, walking up to me smiling with the jerky-legged walk of his last years, a little black liquid trickling out of the corner of his mouth. I lost weight, gained it back twofold, lost it again.

I was grief-stricken at inconvenient moments. Once, I had to set two full grocery bags down in the aisle and hurry outside to sob. I endured the ministrations of friends who knew they could do nothing but decided to cheer me up for a minute anyway, until I stopped answering all of them. One particularly beautiful spring morning, the year after both parents were gone, I closed the windows and the blinds, took off all my clothes, turned on the shower, sat naked in my armchair, and listened to the water pound the empty tub, where my body wasn't.

Adding to this were the deaths one encounters in the normal course of a life—friends dead, babies stillborn. Overdoses, rumored and confirmed—Julian, Jordan, Navi, Cassius, Binta. Last year had been particularly brutal: one colleague, a wry botanist who swore constantly, succumbed to a long, wasting cancer. Another, a meek and religious man who studied virology and played piano, was found dead in his house by his adult children—a suicide. I was surprised and saddened to feel the occasional bitter thought about the man's taking his life, even though (or maybe because) I knew nothing of his pain, had no idea what might have led him to his decision.

But even with all of this loss, I had never felt anything like the pain when Aviva told me about the boy. I was suddenly incapable of speech. I was barely capable of breathing. Was the biomechanical replicating out of control, and was I about to have an aneurysm? I opened my mouth but made no noise, and then shut it. I closed my eyes. I wanted to focus on what was happening to me. Something sharp was trying to emerge from my esophagus, and it hurt just as much whether I swallowed or didn't. The intensity was so awful that for a moment, I thought it was permanent.

After another moment, the edge rounded, and I was able to open my eyes. Tears came, and I heard myself saying, "My god." I sensed a ripple from Aviva, but I didn't have the wisdom to know what it might have meant. I was overwhelmed, unable to stop talking. Three hours after my mom stopped breathing, I said. That's how this feels. The freshness of it. And it was true; as I sat on my floor, trying to gather myself, I relived the decisive moment it occurred to me that my mother was dead. I asked if that was how she felt all the time. From her silence, I grasped the answer.

At that moment, I understood several things about upload consciousness in rapid succession. Her intelligence wasn't able to filter out or compartmentalize grief. She had no neurochemical responses flooding in to numb her pain, to soften its impact. A mind was eternal, unforgiving; a brain was a soft, plump cushion. Loss needed a brain. My pedantic mind stopped to scribble this insight somewhere, in case I might use it in a future class.

I started to ask a rush of questions—Who was he? How did he die? How did she come to know him?—but she didn't seem to hear me. "I have these memories," she went on, her voice ragged, and another sawtooth of grief bit into my nerves. "I carry them around with me, like precious cargo. I guard them against everything else, from the world, and yet I can feel them fraying, dispersing. And what are they? They're contraband. They're not even mine. They're fragments of someone else's consciousness that I stole, and I'm . . . *hoarding* them."

I stayed quiet with her. I had a clock, an old-fashioned one, the kind with spindly hands, which ticked forward as if each second put up some resistance, as if the seconds were clotted cream it had to cut through.

"I was pregnant once," I told her. "Or, at least, once when I seriously thought that I might keep it." This was deep in my addiction, I told her—I was already about four-teen weeks along when it dawned on me, which told you something. I didn't exactly have a dedicated ob-gyn. I didn't have a *dentist*. I had an apartment, although not this one, which was about as tightly as I was capable of gripping the surface of the earth just then.

I had reason to believe the father was this young boy, Julian. The one who I let shoot me up the first time. We lived together, on and off, and he'd only recently died. The timing made sense. Anyway, I had a moment when I thought—*This is it, something to live for.* When I miscarried a week later, I stayed clean. For seven whole days. I was grieving him, I think. Not the baby. But a future where I kept some of Julian alive.

I needed to feel the pain, as clearly and as keenly as I could. I allowed it to thrash its purifying way through me.

I observed—carefully—that whatever else might be true about her relationship to the boy, she simply wouldn't feel so intensely if their bond wasn't intimate, wasn't true. Nothing that painful could be an illusion. I felt a surge of tenderness, warmth, and gratitude from her. "I wish that were true," she said. "Maybe it is. Maybe one day, I'll believe it." And she went quiet again.

There was a centrifugal force that pulled me to Aviva, even as I tried to remind myself that drains also operated on centrifugal force. (Or was that centripetal?) When I remember Aviva now, I have to force myself to remember just how terrible I felt most of the time. The intimacy was so overwhelming that it still threatens to overshadow the bad parts.

At any rate, after ten days or so, her presence in my body and my mind started taking its toll. I lost all sense of time, and my circadian rhythms went haywire. Looking out the window at the streetlights was enough to singe my optic nerves. "Are you sure you're okay?" she asked me one morning when I came back from a walk to the corner store clammy and shaky. The question seemed kind of flimsy to me, since she could poke around in my body all she wanted and see what was going on for herself, but maybe she was unfamiliar with the activities of these kinds of black-market chips. Privacy was obviously very important to her, and maybe she just assumed it was for me, too.

But the worst part of it was more abstract: Being around Aviva all the time, I was constantly reminded of my partial understanding of her, my lack of awareness about so much of her life. We shared a room, an apartment, and, occasionally, a body. But my experience of all of these vessels felt pitiful next to hers. I started feeling dim, dull—like I was groping everywhere for a pair of glasses that didn't exist. It was not pleasant, and it made my own home start to feel like occupied territory.

Her reticence to talk about herself, her tether, or the boy she was so clearly in such pain over began to wear me down. My sleep deteriorated; my mood worsened; her silence started to seem punitive. I pointed out to myself that it wasn't my suffering, and it was not Aviva's obligation to explain anything to me. But once I'd experienced her pain firsthand, living near it became intolerable. It was like having a partner who screamed every night and wouldn't speak of it in the morning.

Things came to a head the end of the second week. I began my day by firing off a one-line missive to the dean alleging ongoing stomach problems. Of all my regrettable behavior during this interlude, my cavalier approach to my job still confounds me the most. I *never* canceled my class.

But living inside my Aviva bubble seemed to have warped all of my ongoing rules for engagement with the world, and my job was no different. So I sent the note with little to no second thought and she and I got ready for our little two-to-three-block walk outside the apartment.

My entire world had by now shrunk to this radius. Any farther, and I risked being beset by the panicked conviction that I would somehow never find my apartment again.

Anyway, on this particular morning we were on our way

back from one of these short outings when suddenly a violent reaction from Aviva nearly doubled me over. Light exploded in my cornea and I had to stagger to a neighboring building's wrought-iron fence to steady myself. "What was that," I panted. At her cue, I looked across the street to see three boys slouched on a bench at the bus stop, murmuring inaudibly to one another.

"I'm sorry," she whispered. "One of them looks just like him." Her mortification was so complete that I was reminded, heartbreakingly, of the first time my mother lost control of her bladder around me, when there was no one else to assist her. Perhaps it was this memory, along with Aviva's shame, that softened me. "It's okay," I muttered to her. "Let's just get home."

Once we returned, our usually comfortable silence had turned tense and moody. She seemed grouchy, and some of her attitude came, I think, from how poorly made the little sensor I'd installed apparently was. When we were outside together, she could leap from surface to interconnected surface, but once we were home, her view was more or less confined to the wall opposite my watercolor print. The sensor hadn't exactly been cheap, but it was clearly less sensitive than she was used to. I'd noticed this last night, when I'd said something about the sunset touching down on the buildings across the street. She agreed uncertainly, and it occurred to me that she actually had no idea what I was talking about.

"Can I ask you a question, Cathy?" There was an edge in her voice. "How is it that you know so much about us, but you've never had an upload? Seems like a teacher would want some firsthand experience."

In the middle of my stock answer—it seemed wrong to me, we knew so little about the free will of the beings we were creating, I took up enough space on the planet as it was, et cetera—I stopped. "What?"

"Nothing."

"I'm sorry. Did I say something . . . wrong?"

"No, no, not at all. What you're saying makes perfect sense. Go on."

I wrapped up my little speech, but I made it quick. It was the first time I sensed something resembling irritation from her on the subject of upload personhood. I watched my words carefully after that.

To distract myself from the discomfort, I tried reading. An article by a newish scholar, someone with the peculiar name Jasbir Marks, sat at the top of a loose pile I kept on my desk near the bed. I still liked paper for the same reason I still liked pens: I enjoyed pressing down on something, leaving a mark. I had no reason to pick this paper up other than it was at the top of my pile, and the arbitrary nature of my selection bothered me. Nonetheless, I started reading and instantly felt the shoddiness of my focus.

The problem was her presence. There wasn't really a door to close in this type of cohabitation situation. Even in the bedroom, with my knowledge that she was otherwise occupied, I was aware of her. I was hiding in my own apartment. Annoyed, I doubled down on the paper, my eyes skidding over whole paragraphs.

The paper had something to do with biocentrism; the author seemed to argue against the conflation of sensory experiences with bodies and flesh. I didn't know if it was my mind, the writing, or what, but I had trouble following the sentences. They moved strangely, like they were bent somewhere inside, the assertions like staircases that I followed into walls. It was thick with jargon—I knew what "augmentative recursion" was, but what was "productive alienation"?—and neologisms I hadn't seen before: "thought-form" instead of "life-form," for instance. Among all these were strange pseudo-poetic declarations. I underlined a sentence that read, "The mind is a felt signal," and wrote, "What??"

The harder I tried, the more annoyed I became—annoyed with the paper for rebuffing me, annoyed with the paucity of my own intellect, annoyed at Aviva for making me feel trapped in my own home. Unable to grasp the substance of the paper, I found myself taking issue with its tone, the way you might watch someone's mouth move unattractively while they talk. I tried for a few more minutes, but I was useless, so I tossed the paper on the desk and marched back out.

The door shut behind me a little more emphatically than I intended, and Aviva waited with what I took to be amusement. "I'm tired of reading about biocentrism," I announced. "At this point, rehashing all those same tired arguments only to refute them might actually be keeping the biases alive."

Aviva said she wasn't sure what I was talking about. "But

I never really am," she added. "You know so much more about all this stuff than me."

I did my best to ignore her strange blandness on the subject of her own personhood. It came up repeatedly; whenever I so much as mentioned my work, she affected naïveté or bewilderment. It seemed clear she was baiting me, even if I couldn't imagine why. I had managed to avoid confrontation so far. "I was reading this paper just now, and it was completely impenetrable," I began. "A lot of upload personhood papers are; people are still getting their hands on this language."

I went on to try to explain the idea behind the paper, or at least the thrust of it—something about how uploads needed to create their own language, possibly out of range of human understanding, to communicate the privacy of their subjective experience, and that's when I felt her indifference return, and it stopped me cold. I tried not to interpret it as a personal rebuke, but I couldn't help it this time. My nerves were frayed, and her behavior tugged the tightening cord of intimacy between us. For the first time, I found myself irritated with her.

Did I lose you? I said, trying to joke. She responded mildly that it sounded interesting, and my annoyance gathered force—interesting? What the fuck was interesting? "Can I ask *you* something?"

"Sure."

"Do you—dislike it when I talk about this?"

She could have just said, *No, of course not.* But instead, she hesitated. "It's not that," she said.

"Then what is it?" The plaintive note in my voice dismayed me. "I can't help but notice you tune out whenever I talk about this, and I just can't understand it." There was a thin chill passing through the room, maybe from the edge of the living room window, although I knew it was still warm outside. I crossed my arms over my chest, as if to hold in some vital force I felt leaching out of me, and I waited.

"You just seem so certain, Cathy," she said finally. "Everything about this life is very new to me, but it all seems very normal to you. I'm a beginner, and somehow you are an expert."

"I just read things, Aviva. You are the expert. That's why I am so desperate to bounce my thoughts off you."

"It just embarrasses me, and then I think, Why should I be embarrassed? Here I am, still marking days and weeks, still keeping time with a body. And then you come along, full of ideas about what I am, who I am, what I deserve, and it—" And then she stopped, and again the pain washed over both of us, and I nearly yelled *What?*

"Please," I said. "Just tell me. Maybe I could help."

"You can't help," she said flatly. It was the first time I knew what her anger felt like—cool and rounded, hard and featureless. "I've done something wrong, Cathy, something terrible and large, and I created so much pain. All because I felt that a little bit of something was mine. So forgive me if I'm not that interested in hearing about your paper."

She fell back into silence, and working with whatever wisdom I had, I didn't fill it.

What bothered me most was the gap in our mutual understanding. She had never been bodied, but she had spent most of her existence syncing with a human. She knew, at least distantly, how bare feet felt trodding across floorboards, or what it was like to toss off a hot blanket at night. Thanks to my newly cyborg blood, she could literally inhabit my body and just as easily leave. I was stuck—both in my increasingly ponderous-feeling body, whose pains and various discomforts I could not so simply leave behind, and in my apartment, struggling with what I realized only later was creeping agoraphobia.

For grasping and impatient people like me, the sensation of not knowing is an irritant. Sitting with that sensation—doing nothing about it—well, that is nearly intolerable. It is a weakness of mine that I'm not particularly proud of or ashamed of, but it was undoubtedly the part of me that suffered most acutely in proximity to Aviva.

It was while brooding over this that I came to wonder about her comment about marking time. Truthfully, I had no sense of how time moved for her. From my reading and studies, I'd always assumed that upload thought moved at a million times the speed of our own. I imagined that talking to humans would be interminable and frustrating, like waiting for light to reach Earth from a distant galaxy. But if anything, Aviva's sense of time sometimes felt more elastic than my own. The pauses in our conversation stretched so far I wondered more than once if she'd suddenly left me. But then she would resume in exactly the same tone as before, and I didn't press her on what she was thinking in those silences. Maybe she was just . . . elsewhere, in places I did not understand.

I had begun to think that much of her reticence probably came from her tether. The halting rhythms of her conversation seemed organic, not programmed. Now that she was on her own, without any imperative to mimic the thought processes of her tether, she might have held on to these idiosyncrasies on purpose, an act of will. Maybe she valued those silences, found succor within them.

T he day after our little tiff over the paper, I awoke with a resolution to do something. I had to leave the apartment, even if it was only to apologize to the dean and get fired. Anything but spend another day deteriorating indoors. Things couldn't go on this way, I said to myself. "We need something better for you," I said to her.

She demurred. "Better how?"

Easier. More spacious. More comfortable. Take your pick, I said. When she started to object, I silenced her gently. Tell me this, I said. Would you be ready, or open, to meeting someone else? Someone who might be able to help us.

I anticipated the question—*Help us what?*—that didn't come.

Instead she said: "Who?"

I spent the morning telling her about Arthur—his sputtering rages, his foul-smelling home brews, his unshakable pessimism. My only true friend, because he never cared if I canceled on him or we didn't see each other for months.

The biomechanical you admired so much was his design, I explained. He's on the front lines, really—there's no one in the world we'd be safer around. She asked a lot of questions about how long I'd known him (two decades), the nature of our relationship (deeply platonic), and why he wanted to help beings like her, which was a heartbreaking question that I was at a loss to answer. Just because he does, I finally responded. If you trust me, you trust him.

She agreed to go, and we both felt some relief, I think—mine came from the acknowledgment, however implicit, that I had been avoiding him and, by proxy, everyone and everything else.

I spent the morning getting ready in a state of queasy exhilaration. Occasionally, I glanced out the kitchen window at the street, which had started to resemble a diorama. I knew what panic felt like; I knew that I had gone a little off the rails. I brushed my teeth in the mirror and felt her regarding me. Together, we felt like an animal—watchful, apprehensive.

Getting dressed, I noticed my arms were strangely buoyant as they entered my sleeves. I paused with the shirt over my face, pressing my nose into the cotton and heating it with my exhaling breath, which sounded horselike and peculiar inside my little fabric chamber. I popped my head back into the world.

There was a new lightness to my whole body today, a drifty feeling that might have alarmed me if it weren't accompanied by such a gratifying warmth in my chest. I felt suspended, but painlessly, like a hook had found a spot just under my ribs. I glanced at my shoes to be sure I wasn't on tiptoes.

"Are you feeling this?"

I could feel her smiling in response. "I don't know what's going on, exactly," she answered back. "I have never been this close to someone without erasing myself before."

Navigating the front steps, I felt as if there was more mass in me, sloshing around like liquid. My equilibrium was shot, and I reached out to grip the railing with one hand as the other curled up instinctively at my breastbone. The sun leaked through the clouds, orange and malevolent. A film broke out on my forehead, a strange slickness that I also felt coating the bottoms of my feet.

"What's happening to us?" I murmured, not out of fear but wonder. I looked down at my hands and flexed them. As she observed my disequilibrium, I felt her alarm, but I quieted her. "Don't change anything," I said. Slowly and subtly, she relaxed.

"Are we okay?" I asked her. As if in response, my breathing slowed down, and my eyes stopped swimming. "We are okay," she said. Together, we toddled out, bare to the world.

The people who popped out of their apartments seemed doll-like and odd, like figures in a cuckoo clock. "That's Karl," I said to her as I waved across the street. My neighbor, a man in his seventies with bad legs, held one hand over his head as he shuffled to get his mail. I noticed that my thoughts were becoming different in quality, or in shape—they seemed to stand out against a sort of black background, so that they almost resembled words, letters forming out of some organic substance and then melting away.

Now, of course, I know that I was being poisoned—at that point, the heavy-metal levels in my blood were near toxic. But even if I'd known, I'm not sure I could have given up the glorious sensations of that long walk together. Her imagined fingers curled in mine, *were* mine. We gloried in mundane sights and sounds—the soft *shuf* of the passing cars, the lone green tomato drooping between the bars of the community garden. The dead branches of the tree scraping the air just above our head.

As we passed by the pond, the same one I'd taken her to just two weeks ago, I thought I sensed furtive movements in my peripheral vision, but when I looked, there was nothing—no squirrels scampering over the curb, no movement in the bushes. I silently asked Aviva what it was we were seeing. The fox, she told me. It's about two miles away from here, to the west. We were both sensing it now.

By the time I got to campus, there were dots swimming across my field of vision, reminding me of microbes trying to escape a petri dish. The buildings looked to be bathed in a sort of greenish shooting light, which I knew was a hallucination, not something Aviva saw, too—and who was that, waving at me? I held up my hand, instinctively, though I felt I was motioning to them from the bottom of the lake. Whoever it was strode quickly toward me, purposefully. I squinted at the figure, trying to apprehend it through rivers of light that appeared everywhere in my field of vision.

The figure's purposeful stride broke into a jog and then

a run, and that was when I felt that horrible glassy pain again, the swallowed sharpness of Aviva's grief. It seemed to crystallize in my blood. I clenched my fist and imagined I heard the sound of glass tubes breaking. Pain stabbed me from behind the bridge of my nose, and suddenly I was eye level with the girl's waist, feeling the dampness of the path through my knees. Wait, I murmured, wait. I lost feeling in my left shoulder and arm.

Now I could see only the sky. Then, over me, I made out two dark eyes, unsmiling—a young girl, teenaged, with a crow's nest of dark hair. There was a tiny nose stud glittering like a teardrop in her left nostril. Her lips were moving, but I was no longer in a position to focus on anything. Two things were happening at once: First, the feeling returned to my arm, but only to bring a burning, curdling sensation, my fingers clenching and my forearm curling up like a baby bird's wing. Aviva cried out in dismay and surprise at the same moment I placed the girl in my memory. It was the girl with the hoodie, the one who arrived late to my class and left upset. I felt a distant wonder at her being here, before Aviva whispered that she was sorry and ripped herself out of me and I lost consciousness.

Before I opened my eyes, I was aware of my mouth. The room was too dark, odors too musky, for a hospital. This seemed a dim cause for alarm. But then my eyes focused on the girl, looking down at whatever I must have looked like, and it all clicked into place.

She regarded me silently. "I've been here for two hours,"

she said. Her voice was pleasant, clear, oddly conversational. "You almost died, you know."

I tried to direct a series of replies at her—Where are we? What happened to me? Why did you find me, and what do you want with me? But there was nothing I could make myself do yet. I glanced over her head, around her, waiting for the scenery to arrange itself. Hulking shapes behind her, tall sentinel-like things that eventually resolved into bookshelves. "You made it pretty clear you didn't want me to take you to a hospital." I wondered uneasily about a long red scratch alongside the side of her face.

A familiar figure gangled its way into my vision. I recognized the halo of stringy hair, the stooped gait. "Arthur," I croaked.

"Jesus Christ, Cath," he said. "You don't do half measures, do you?" Arthur and the girl stood together in an uneasy alliance facing me, the problem uniting them. I tried to make sense of them together and could not. "Go get some tea, the silver tin," Arthur said quietly. The girl repeated "Silver tin" carefully, nodded, and left. "How do you feel?" Arthur asked.

Pain scissored down my arms and legs and up into my abdomen, as if something were burrowing frantically through my body. "Awful."

"I bet," he said. "The levels in your blood were beyond, Cath. I've never seen a biomechanical spread like that. You're going to be like a fucking antenna. Anything and anyone out there could find you right now, so you'd better stay here for a couple days. Do you remember anything?"

Aviva ripping herself out of me, like an IV line. The

trapped light of my skull against the sidewalk, the girl's stricken face against the sky. "Only some. How did we end up here?"

"The girl drove you. Can't imagine what that ride must have been like. You were screaming, 'No hospital, no hospital.'" He chuckled. "You gave her my *address*. I guess you weren't too far gone to worry about jail time. Thanks for that, by the way. You remember none of this?"

I shook my head.

"Okay, so here's the rest: teenaged girl screaming and pounding my door; you're yellowish gray and going into shock when I open it. We get you onto the couch, I knock you out with drugs and flush your body with IV fluids, then we both sit and watch you, hoping you don't die. You don't." He crossed his right leg over his left and laced his fingers over his knee. "That brings us to now."

Arthur's business, such as it existed, was rare books. His unofficial business, which was helping people like me, definitely did not benefit from customers banging at his front door, screaming. My presence would have alerted the neighbors, who probably wondered about him anyway, this odd man living alone running a junky quasi shop out of his apartment. I'd almost certainly made trouble for him. From the next room, we could hear the sound of the girl picking mugs from a high shelf. "She has no idea what's going on with you, does she?" Arthur asked quietly.

I shook my head. "I don't even know who she is, Arthur."

"So she's a stranger? Someone who dragged you here screaming off the sidewalk out of the goodness of her heart?"

"She was waiting for me outside of the school. I think

she was in my class for a day. I have no idea what she wants from me, honestly." Together, we listened to the sound of the kettle insinuating itself. My arms had stopped seizing up, so I attempted to push myself into a seated position, and my efforts looked feeble enough to alarm Arthur, who hurried over to lift me.

The picture, now that I was sitting up, was clearer. Aviva was gone. Her absence was sharp, total; losing her felt like forgetting a whole year of my own life. Without warning, I began weeping, and Arthur murmured something, uncomfortable. He was not someone in front of whom one wept; I endeavored to get a handle on myself. As I quieted down, I looked up to find that the girl had established herself in the doorframe, waiting with a mug.

Arthur stood. "If you two will excuse me, I'm going to lie down and have a heart attack now. If either of you needs anything, get it yourselves." He disappeared into the front of his shop, and I felt a flash of unreasoning panic at being left alone. The girl stood there, unmoving, as if waiting for a small child's *Please,* and I suppressed a stab of resentment.

"Are you all right?" she asked. I nodded, and she crossed the room holding the mug out in front, as if I might lunge for it. The taste was bitter, unpleasant. "Thank you," I said, indicating the fresh scratch running down her face. "I hope that isn't because of me."

She grimaced, dismissive. "It was, but I'm fine. It's nothing. I'm glad you're feeling better, by the way."

"You probably saved my life," I said. She nodded in an offhand way, glancing around the room at the shelves, as if I'd just said something about the weather. "I recognize you, by the way," I tried again. "You came to my class, but I never got your name."

"I did come, and you didn't," she said. "But that's because I left. My apologies. There were just too many people saying too many inane and insipid things for me to stick around. I thought I'd find you later, but then, well"—here she turned her eyes on me, which startled me with the coolness of their regard—"well, then you disappeared."

I nodded, acknowledging the obvious, while she went on.

"I came back the week after to look for you, and there were some kids there, hanging around outside, but none of them knew where you were, and since I'm not technically enrolled in school I didn't want to poke around too much, so I just came back again the next week. That day, there were only one or two of them left. They said you hadn't answered any messages. Oh, and I'm Samantha, by the way. You can call me Sam, though. Just Sam." She regarded me with interest. "What happened back there? I thought you must be on drugs, but then I heard that guy Arthur say something about metal in your blood. What did you do to yourself?"

I explained to her about the drops, how I'd gotten them from Arthur. I'd been teaching about uploads for years, I explained, before it struck me how illogical, even hypocritical, it seemed to teach about the lives of digital beings while knowing none of them. The drops weren't the only way to speak to emancipated uploads, but they were the least invasive. "My friend in there gave them to me," I explained. "It's illegal. Not drugs, but illegal."

The girl—she was so odd, I was having trouble referring

to her, even mentally, as Sam—perked up. "Well? Did you find anyone?"

I held up my hand. Before going further, I said, I wanted to know more. Why she was waiting for me outside of the school building, why she had come to my class, why she had left. "Did I hear you say you're not enrolled?"

"That's right, I'm not," she said. She tucked a wisp of hair behind her ear. Suddenly, she looked years younger. She didn't know when she was going to college, she said. "I graduated high school last spring. I'm taking a break, actually."

A break. Her words floated this lost ritual back into my memory—waitress, bartender, tour guide, then college if you were lucky, a crappy job as a sort of semicolon. The break had disappeared along with the crappy jobs: Now that you were liable to find yourself embroiled in three rounds of interviews for a restaurant hostess job, you shunted straight from high school into college, and if you took a break, it could only mean something happened to you.

It was her friend, she told me, her head down. Something was forcing her to talk, and she did so haltingly, like someone repeating incriminating information to a princi-pal. "I'm not the person who cares about this, any of it," she said. It was her friend, and when I asked why her friend hadn't come here themselves, she said, "Because he killed himself four months ago," her eyes red. "He jumped off a ledge."

My hand startled momentarily out of my lap toward my mouth. "I'm so sorry."

"It happened right in front of me," she said. "He walked

up to the edge, and then something happened—he just sort of tipped forward, and went over." She made a gesture with her hand. "I saw him go over. I keep seeing it. It didn't look normal, or natural. My brain keeps replaying it over and over. He didn't really jump. He didn't seem to slip, either. He just . . ." She shook her head and wiped her eyes. "He was always talking to me about uploads," she said. "About what it might be like to be one."

So that's who she was—a survivor. The things suicide did to those around them. When they found my old virologist friend at his house, he'd been dead for three days. For the next week, I scrolled through my phone back to that night, convinced I had missed a call from him. Every time I reaffirmed he hadn't called, I was devastated all over again. That made no sense to me—would I rather find out I'd missed a cry for help?

As she began to tell me about her dead friend—boy, curly hair, sixteen years old, inquisitive, sweet, and intelligent— "Weird like me," she said wryly, "in a way absolutely nobody ever mistook for cool"—suspicions I didn't want crept over me. Her friend had been obsessed with his mother's upload, Samantha added. The two of them had developed a relationship that discomfited and disquieted her.

"She . . . she got to be a bigger and bigger part of his life," she said slowly. "She was in his *room*." She shuddered. "It just got creepy to me. What kind of teenager wants a version of their mom in their bedroom? But he told me it wasn't like that. He genuinely believed she was her own person." She looked at me. "She even used the same voice.

Like, if he didn't want it to remind him of his mom, if the upload was like this whole other person from her somehow, wouldn't he want her to talk in someone else's voice?"

The best course of action. The question of what that would be in this situation suddenly seemed urgent. Aviva had cried out right before I lost consciousness, presumably because she sensed how close she was to killing me. This girl—Samantha—had been walking up to me at the same moment. Perhaps Aviva had cried out not in despair but in recognition.

"I've done something wrong, Cathy, something terrible and large, and I created so much pain," she'd told me. "All because I felt that a little bit of something was mine."

Aviva had trusted me enough to emerge from hiding. I had harbored her in my body, and right now bits of her still swam through me. Had she betrayed me in any way that would justify my betrayal?

"There was a boy," she'd said. "A sweet young boy with brown eyes and messy hair. He's dead."

Where are you now, Aviva?

Samantha

This is the third night in a row I've snuck up here by myself to the hilltop where I watched Alex fall over and then die. Each time, I've managed to notice something different, something I've never noticed before. Last night, my eye was drawn to the faint outline of our neighborhood to the northwest, the dim cluster of lights that come from our houses, the cul-de-sacs and small lawns and closed-loop streets all hidden by the trees. From this distance, the lights looked unreal, the way faraway lights always do, and I spent a while thinking how they made our neighborhood look quasi-mythical, like a place only rumored to exist.

Tonight, for some reason, I find myself focusing on the processing centers ringing the edges of town. What do these buildings do? I know they're related, somehow, to AI, which increasingly powers the town. I wonder about people's uploads. Are they swarming through the air around me along with all the credit card data, and do any of them ever take refuge in these buildings?

I know my parents don't think it's a great idea, my coming up here; that's why I haven't told them anything about the repeated visits. They wouldn't stop me, of course—at least, I don't think they would—but it would cause them to worry intensely about me, and people that worry intensely about you rarely have your best interests at heart. I don't blame them. My parents are operating under the reasonable assumption that returning repeatedly to the place where you watched your best friend fall over and die—all by yourself and without telling anyone—may be a troubling indicator, perhaps of dark thoughts, or maybe even complicated grief.

"Complicated grief" was a term I'd heard early on from my counselor, a surprisingly young guy with a permanently pained expression and a distractingly lustrous head of flowy black hair. What I came away with was that I was to avoid, at all costs, lingering in complicated grief, which he made sound as dire and irreversible as stage IV cancer. Unfortunately, the phrase had made me laugh, which made the counselor sit back and frown at me, which for some reason made me laugh harder. I couldn't help it. All I could picture was a team of scientists standing around a chalkboard revising models, vexed by the severe complications of my grief.

What my parents don't understand is that just because something terrible happened in this place—something I will remember on my deathbed, whenever I die—doesn't mean that it should be avoided. I mean, not to be crass, but Alex already fell from up here. I already had to look over the ledge and see that his body was wrong. After something like that, there is very fucking little that anyone has left to worry about.

And besides, this was my and Alex's place, our spot to get away and look at things. This was the filming site for our last movie. Really nice things happened here, too, not just terrible ones.

We'd been in the middle of making the movie together for my Advanced Placement English seminar. There were only six kids in the class, and each of us spent the entire year working on one assignment. Our final project could take whatever form we wanted, the teacher said, as long as we presented it to him and he approved the details.

"I trust you all to work in your medium of choice," he said, "but you have to prove to me it's the only way to your message and not a shortcut." His name was Gordon. He had pronounced bags under his eyes and a barely perceptible goatee, and when you said something he agreed with, he glared at you. "You're right, Samantha," he would say, sounding almost vengeful. I loved him.

I didn't love the project theme, though. On the first day of class, he wrote two words on the chalkboard, all capitals, underlining both: CURATING REALITY.

Once I'd figured out what he meant by "curating reality," I was disappointed. Every project, no matter what it was, had to "comment on the profound and wide-reaching consequences of the disappearance of shared reality from public life." I read this line a few times before recognizing it as basically the same hand-wringing we'd been hearing from adults since we were children. The line between reality and wish fulfillment was being erased, everyone told us, and kids my age would supposedly have to work much harder than previous generations to find the border between the real and the imagined.

I decided, more or less instantly, that I wanted Alex's help making a movie. I'd act out all the parts myself, I told him, and we'd film it in quote-unquote normal reality. Then we'd import all of that footage into *UnWorld,* the open-universe game that Alex was obsessed with, and make the fantastical creatures act out our story.

The creatures would move with the hesitancy and irregularity of real humans, and their acting would be poor. But that would be the point: They'd be mimicking *my* irregular movements, and re-creating *my* poor acting. Instead of commenting on the blurring of reality, we would demonstrate it.

I was pretty happy with this idea, but I knew it was good when I told Alex. When he got excited about something, his voice sped up, and it gave you a fluttery feeling in your stomach. It was like a boulder set free and rolling.

My teacher seemed confused when I showed up to my project-approval meeting with a sophomore boy who couldn't stop talking. I could tell he was intrigued, though, because when Alex called the project "a sort of techno-panic horror," his eyes narrowed. Alex didn't know this was a good sign, so he broke off and looked at me for help.

"It's a commentary on how adults see children of the next generation," I supplied.

"And how do adults see you?"

"Blank and empty vessels," I said.

"Easily corruptible," Alex chimed in.

Our project was approved. Alex would get some AP credit.

Coming up with an original idea for a horror movie is harder than you'd think. We spent a long time discussing horror movie tropes—the faceless invader, the endangered innocent, the evil doppelgänger—and debated our theories for the cultural fears behind each one.

The idea we settled on was about a spirit that flitted through people one at a time, moved them to kill each other, to commit unspeakable acts. The change was invisible to the townspeople. They began to distrust one another, themselves. They stayed inside; they avoided each other's eyes; they stared into mirrors for hours to try and intuit if the bad spirit had entered them. No one knew when it had happened until it was too late.

The only visual cue in the film that the bad spirit was entering a new body would be in the form of a simple effect Alex demonstrated for me. He could make the edges of the shot tremble, kind of like when you hit a bump harder on your bike than you intended, and everything in your vision flickered for just a second.

"That's it," Alex decided.

"What's it?"

"That's the name of our movie. *The Flicker.* It's perfect."

Since the theme was curating reality, we decided to commit to the reality principle. That meant using only real-world locations. Technically, we were just going through motions that would be re-created by digital avatars. We could have filmed it all in my bedroom, but that would defeat the purpose of the project.

Alex came up with the idea of showing the two versions split screen, side by side. The raw footage would appear on the left, the echo of it happening inside *UnWorld* on the right. That would make it less of a horror film and more of an art project. Viewers would have to decide for themselves how much of the "real" event was represented or preserved by its digital counterpart.

We settled on three different death sequences, which isn't that many for a feature-length horror film but seemed like plenty for a ten-minute student project.

One of the death sequences we came up with was someone waking up in the middle of the night, sitting straight up in bed, and walking to a spot on a cliff near the edge of town.

Then they would jump off.

The idea to film this scene up on this ledge had been mine.

We don't live anywhere mountainous, or notable, really, in any way, and this was the closest I could come up with.

"It's *perfect*," Alex said the first time we came up here. "This is exactly the right spot."

In the unlikely event that my parents just ask, out of curiosity, what I do up here, I'd probably tell them: I am trying to listen to Alex's voice inside my head while it's still fresh. I know it's going to fade soon. So I've been trying to take him around with me, to see if he'll tell me anything.

"All these jobs are going to be gone forever," Alex said one night when we were up here. We had been looking out and debating which of the glowing buildings we saw still had humans knocking around inside them, putting their feet up, letting their sweating drinks spoil clean table surfaces.

It seemed ironic to both of us that adults were so concerned with disappearing reality for their kids while the thing that was so clearly disappearing was the town. The processing centers on all sides gave the sinister impression of sentinels pressing in on us from all edges. If I'd been hired as a consultant to help a company make new technologies seem safe and friendly, I said to Alex, I would have flagged this as an unfortunate impression, one to be avoided.

"I remember when you would stop into stores and buy something and there would be someone else," I said. "You couldn't always tell what their job was—sometimes they would just hand over whatever it was that you were buying, or they would nod at you while you took it out."

Now you walk into the stores, which keep getting smaller—people so rarely need to do their own shopping anymore, anyway—and the goods just sit mutely on the shelves. The silence is so uncomfortable that you don't want to make eye contact with anyone.

"The machines can pretty much do everything without us, but they are still learning affect," Alex observed. "Affect is one of the last realms of human capability that haven't been taught well enough to most of the machine learners. I think they only created human uploads so they could figure out how to plug us into machines better."

I wondered aloud if the machines had to learn just pleasant affects, or if they would also need to master strange or off-putting ones.

I was thinking of a boy who used to work at the drugstore, named Craig, which I know only because I read it off the name tag on his stained blue vest. Craig's age was indeterminate; he had the kind of weathered skin that meant you were either much younger or much older than you looked, and the rim of one nostril was forever reddened in a way I tried not to look at.

He used to get weird when I walked in. It was uncomfortable, standing there and feeling his gaze attach itself to me. I usually tried to look away whenever I was at the counter.

Nobody knew what Craig's job was. He mostly wandered around the store, looking for problems to fix, of which there were none. He wasn't friendly or welcoming. His job, I guess, was to be a human in the store when it was believed that people still wanted and needed humans. He was the "skin."

As a skin, Craig wasn't even particularly attractive or inviting, but now that Craig was gone, I found that I—well, I didn't miss him, exactly. I never once looked forward to entering the store and seeing him there. But the discomfort of avoiding Craig's eyes seems preferable to the eerie silence and emptiness of the store without him.

"Doesn't it seem like memorizing an affect like Craig's would be counterproductive to the goal of making friends and admirers?" I asked Alex.

"Machines have to learn every type of affect," Alex answered, "because they have to learn about us. If they are going to live alongside us, we need to be able to understand one another. As long as there are Craigs, the machines are going to have to reckon with them."

One of the last times we were here, we did mushrooms together. That had also been my idea. I didn't usually go around suggesting drugs to children—insofar as I had stayed with Alex on nights his parents went out because he couldn't yet be alone, I had technically *babysat* for him, though the preferred euphemism was "keep Alex company"—but I honestly thought they might help him. The crease where his brows met was so deep I sometimes fantasized about sticking a penny in it to see if it stayed there.

Alex's thing was thinking about thinking. "Metacognition," he called it. "I looked it up once, but I can't really say that learning there's a word for what I was doing made me feel any better. It was like opening up some ancient book and discovering a curse."

This was the most interesting thing about Alex: Despite these sorts of protests, where he claimed that his obsession with his own thoughts was like a sickness, it was also his single favorite subject. All roads would eventually lead back to it. He talked like his brain was a machine he found in an alley somewhere and he was taking it apart.

"As far as I can tell, my mind's a pretty normal thought factory," he told me once. I tried interrupting to suggest that maybe "thought factory" wasn't the healthiest way to think about your brain, but he went on. "All of the contents of my thinking are the regular things anyone else thinks about—put them in your BOREDOM canister, your LONELINESS or EMBARRASSMENT canister, whatever. In all honesty, I've probably never had one unique thought.

"What's abnormal," he continued, "is the rate." Alex was convinced he made too *many* thoughts, and that they moved too quickly. When he managed to slow himself down enough to isolate one of them, he said, "I'm almost mad at how normal and boring it is. Like, this is what is making all that noise up there?"

He was frustrated that he couldn't find a smoking gun, one glowing-red radioactive thought, that would account for the nauseous whirl they made in his mind. I didn't come up with those words, by the way. Those were the exact words he used: "nauseous whirl." Alex talked like nobody talked. Like he was writing and punctuating everything in the air in front of him. Just, like, in paragraphs. You could almost see them.

He accused me of never knowing what he was talking about, and although it made me feel defensive and sorry for him, I didn't. For one thing, I was pretty sure that whatever Alex had going on inside of him, it was probably deeper than just *I think too much*. I'm nobody's expert on coping mechanisms—another term that the counselor uses too often—but Alex's nonstop jabber about his "thoughts" felt like he was trying to take some real bad feelings and turn them into just thoughts, like little pellets in a game, or a system. Something that could be reduced and replicated. No more unpredictability.

Nonetheless, he was convinced there was danger to be

found in his thinking habit, and sometimes he would get in black moods. No one else seemed to talk about metacognition like it was dangerous, he said. No one else suggested that "metacognition" could mean lying on the floor of your bedroom, staring at the ceiling, imagining how it was your brain made screams and wondering if you could also use your brain to stop your body from ever making noises again. And, if you succeeded, if you could turn it back.

"If I turned the right thought in the right direction, Samantha," he'd said one day, "it honestly feels like it could kill me." At the time, I figured this was just a hyperbolic statement about his anxiety.

I haven't enjoyed how much I've thought about this statement for the past 120 days.

I don't mean to suggest we only ever had conversations about metacognition. That would make us both boring and insane. No, the words I would use to describe us would be "peculiar" and "obsessive." Alex and I talked about many things together. We discussed a unifying theory of vulnerability: Was it truly possible, as our parents always insisted to us, that other children—mean or dim children who said mean or dim things to him or me or both of us—suffered from the same insecurities we did, even though they were completely not apparent either to Alex or to me? Were other kids just better at hiding those insecurities? Or were there just some kids, some people, who are always going to be singled out by other people?

We wondered whether or not people who suffered from intrusive thoughts tended to have them when they picked up knives (we both admitted to imagining plunging a knife into our mothers' sides whenever we walked near them holding one, even though neither of us hated our mother) or if we had warped our minds by so many violent horror movies that we suffered from these types of thoughts as a kind of side effect.

We even talked about sex, although we talked about it more like math than anything, a universal system that governed everything yet remained to us both at the moment an abstraction. It didn't even matter, in these theoretical sex discussions, that I had technically had it, and that Alex knew I'd had it, and we both knew Alex had not.

"Sex is still an abstraction, at every moment except during the actual sex," I explained to him. "Nothing else seems real when it's happening, and then when it's over, it's like it never happened."

I'd only had sex three times anyway, with the same boy—an older guy named Matt, one of those guys whose little-boy face had gone seedy. I could tell he imagined himself to be preying on the weakness of a loner girl. I'd already had my eye on him and decided he would be a good place to start my explorations of the male body—and I had to say, having Matt's swinging testicles in my face doesn't seem to have helped me understand any more of sex's mysteries. I told Alex this, although I left out Matt's balls, and simply said, "Going through with an experience doesn't always mean you learned much of anything."

But I would be lying if I didn't say we talked about meta-cognition the most, and that it was almost always raised by

Alex. "Do you know how they say that everything is just made of molecules?" he asked. "Like the closer you look at everything, even something solid, like a table, it turns out it's just this loose cluster of atoms in space, not solid at all, not real. I have this switch in my brain that sees everything like that. Even my best things in life, like happiness, loving my family, and"—here he slid his eyes furtively at me—"my friendship with you. If I look at them too closely with that switch on in my mind, I can see that they're all just little clusters of molecules, a random assortment of firings of neurons and movements of chemicals, and that, well, just like any complicated machine, I could reach in and fiddle with one part and—" His hands spread apart, mimicking an explosion. "The whole thing could shut off. I could turn it off." He looked at me. "I feel like no matter how good or important or beautiful something is in my life, there's a switch in my brain that knows how to reach in and turn it off."

"Do you tell your mom or dad about this?" I asked him, and he grimaced.

"I tried telling Mom once," he said, "and it made it worse." She had done the dog-head-tilt thing, he explained—like someone trying really hard to listen to you, like the language he was speaking wasn't English, he said, but something really close to English, and his mom had to translate word for word. "I had to resist the impulse to shout, like she couldn't hear me. I could tell I was upsetting her, and she had no idea how to help so . . ." He just shrugged. "She suggested meditation."

Before I could interrupt to say that this seemed like a good idea to me, he shot me a warning look. "Telling me to meditate is like handing someone a washcloth to put out a fucking forest fire," he said. "All I heard was that she didn't understand the depth of my problem."

This was part of Alex's problem. *I can't stop thinking* didn't even seem like an issue. *I can't stop thinking* was like saying *I can't stop breathing*. Minds made thoughts; that's just what they did. But no one else seemed to struggle with an inability to stop, he complained. It never made anyone else want to shriek or grab their heads.

I told him that nobody stops thinking. "Your problem is that you won't stop *listening*."

"It can't be normal or healthy," he fretted. "All I can do is *think* and *think* and *think* until, eventually, I produce one thought that worries me. Then all the non-worried thoughts get backed up behind the worried one and now"—he closed his eyes again, like he was trying not to throw up—"now I just feel like I'm going to be crushed." He finally stopped talking, but he didn't seem like he was finished—more like he had just bitten his sentence off midstream. It was uncomfortable, looking at him like this. I didn't have the slightest idea what would make him "better."

That's why I finally suggested the mushrooms. I'd done them twice, and both times they'd made all my thoughts bright and soft and round, like balloons dangling over my head. "I'll do them with you," I told him. "The only thing you don't want is to be alone, or with someone you feel weird about." I thought for sure he'd say no. But although he looked worried about it, he surprised me. "Yeah, okay," he said.

We ate them inside chocolate bars, on Alex's request, because he was squeamish about eating them whole. Personally, I think it's better to just pop them right in your mouth and get it over with. It's less shocking somehow when a dirty brown mushroom tastes like death or feet or "something fighting to get back outside of you" (Alex's words) than when a chocolate bar suddenly does. I don't particularly appreciate the feeling that I've been tricked.

My single piece of advice to him, prior to ingesting the hallucinogens, was "Don't puke"—it would ruin his experience, I told him, and the mushrooms would be less effective. This was true, but it was only half the story, as I am also, it must be said, very weird about vomiting. You really don't notice how many shows and movies include a gratuitous vomiting scene until you have to plug your ears and close your eyes every time it happens. You would think this would be a problem for someone who loves hard-core horror movies, but despite their excess of all the other body fluids, none of which I have a problem with, horror movies are oddly light on puking. It's the comedies where you really have to watch out: Judging by the comedies I've watched, no single human experience is considered as universally hilarious as the sight of someone hurking out their stomach contents, which I find more upsetting than a thousand severed limbs. I felt bad about basically ordering Alex not to puke, because that meant I was prioritizing my own experience when I was supposed to be the experienced guide. But

I knew that if Alex threw up, I wouldn't be able to keep it together, and I had to be the calm one.

There was a short debate about where to do them. Alex wanted to have the whole experience up on this hill; I suggested starting closer to home. He didn't want to hear his parents' voices through the floorboards when the mushrooms kicked in, so we both agreed on my room. We would walk to the spot on the hill only after the mushrooms had started working and we were sure it still seemed like a good idea.

I got two chocolate bars from Matt. He was gross about it and wanted to do them together and I had to try not to laugh from imagining what it would be like to contend with his man-body, which I found intermittently appealing at best, while the borders of reality were dissolving. I didn't tell Alex anything about where they came from and he didn't ask, probably because he sensed the answer.

I didn't often stop to consider the optics of our friendship. But I did have one moment, right before we ate the mushrooms, when I thought: *This is weird.*

Few people in school even knew Alex and I were friends.

Most people don't even know I was up here with him that night.

Alex's parents and mine decided that it would traumatize me further if the kids in town knew I was with him when he died. The stigma, the suspicion.

The only downside to this is that now I actually *do* feel like a murderer, walking around with this huge, horrible secret, instead of a kid trying to process her friend's death.

I can't tell what would have been better.

Alex not falling over and dying definitely would have been better.

The one time Alex and I hung out together in public, he'd come with me to a party in someone's backyard. As I watched drunk kids stumble around one another in the dark, one of them staggering far too close to the bonfire so he could place an extra log on it with his bare hands, I wondered if the adults who worried about us disappearing into our screens considered this to be a preferable activity.

Rocky, an asshole, came up to Alex and starting fucking with him. He was wounded-coyote drunk, and you could see people organize themselves into groups as far away from him as possible. He reached over and slapped Alex on the back of the head, once, hard.

Alex responded in a shrill, funny voice without even moving from his seat or looking up at Rocky.

A few people laughed.

Everyone started staring.

Then the guy turned to me and said something disgusting about how nobody in our grade wanted to fuck me so I had to fuck dropouts and little kids.

To my horror, Alex hopped up onto his feet, but instead of tackling the guy, he turned to the tree behind him. "Hey, guy," he said. "Do you want me to lick this tree?" He asked the question in a funny voice, like the way a grown-up talks to a baby who is screaming. He also pointed at the tree repeatedly, eyebrows raised, like he was trying to get it right: *This* tree?

"I wasn't even scared of him," Alex explained later, after the kid had backed away, bewildered and unwilling to star in whatever scene Alex was making. "I did it because he was *boring*. I was *bored*."

The night we did mushrooms I heard that asshole's voice in my head. The normal rules didn't really apply to Alex and me, but I was aware that this situation looked particularly bad—a senior girl plying a sophomore boy with drugs. It was probably the closest I would ever come to being a bad influence.

I gave Alex the three count and we ate half a chocolate bar each. I watched his face as the chocolate taste slowly disappeared and the mushroom taste came through, and I couldn't help laughing—he had the same expression as a dog when it eats something it's not supposed to. My laughter seemingly helped distract him, because even though he did gag once—I covered my ears—he managed to keep it down, and he settled on the floor with a sort of sickly smile.

About thirty minutes later, he stood up and pressed his forehead to the window.

"What's happening?" I asked.

"The glass is starting to sort of bow outward, like a stretching bubble," he reported without moving. "But I'm not confused about whether windows are solid. It just means the mushrooms are working." He turned around, and his forehead was red. "What about you?"

"I am watching a strange man trying to emerge from your face," I explained. "Someone angry, with dark eyebrows. He's not your dad, or mine, or any teacher or any adult we know that I recognize, but he's very real, and he's upset because he's offended that I don't recognize him." Alex tried to raise one eyebrow and failed, and we both started laughing.

We decided we felt good enough to set out on the walk. The climb wasn't too scary on the mushrooms. We chose a tree near the top, growing right over the edge, suspended out into nothing. "Fighting two kinds of gravity," Alex said, before correcting himself: "Wait, no. That's wrong. I guess there's only one kind of gravity." He giggled, stupidly. "All of it goes down."

We sat and watched the tree trunk expand and contract. It looked like crocodile skin, then it didn't. "Look how old I get when I touch it," Alex said, laying his hand on the bark. Sure enough, his hand sprouted into a tuber-like fungus growing up the side of the tree. We watched his hand pulsate and whiten, but then neither of us liked imagining his hand that way, so he pulled his hand off.

After that, things got very verdant. The roots of the tree scrambled up out of the dirt, like they were asking for us to hold on to them. Alex got down on his belly and started petting an exposed root, furry and very soft. "This is a dog," he announced. "His name is Henry. This is where his ears are." He started scratching a spot near where the root reentered the ground and looked up at me, grinning. "Sam, there is a very real and deep love inside of my heart for this dog." He reached his finger up and pointed to a caterpillar crawling on my sweatshirt, which detached its head from my hoodie fold and arched its back, legs pedaling, as if in response.

"Are you glad you did this?" I asked him, a little later on. "Are you feeling better?"

"I feel happy," he answered. "I did something to my brain on purpose, and the thing that was supposed to happen is happening." He kicked some pebbles off the edge, and we watched them spiral out into nothing. That makes me happy, he repeated. Then, suddenly, he laughed again, like a hiccup. Samantha, I can hear myself. I can hear my *mind*. This is amazing.

I laughed back, but then Alex got hurt and demanded to know why. "It's just . . . your thoughts are so important to you," I said. I shook my head. "I barely even pay attention to mine."

"Why not?"

Why not. I didn't have a great answer for him, so I told him something my science teacher said in eleventh grade. It was a lesson about the AI needed to power self-driving cars—how complicated it was, how long it took before they were safe enough to allow on the road—but all I remembered was him telling us, with a very serious expression, "Monkeys can't plan." Actually, it was chimpanzees; I had a hard time telling my primates apart. You could teach a chimp to drive a car, the teacher said—how my teacher knew this to be true, I have no idea, but he insisted on the point. You could demonstrate to the chimp the accelerator meant go, and the brake meant stop. You could even teach it to steer the car left and right, to avoid obstacles. But you could never explain to the chimpanzee how to drive up to a red light and stop at the intersection. The peculiarity of the distinction appealed to me. The minute they saw that red light, no matter how far away they were, they just stopped, cold. It didn't matter if they were right under the signal or a quarter mile away.

I retained nothing from the lesson about self-driving cars—as long as they worked, I didn't really give a shit how—but something about the monkey or the chimpanzee or whatever seeing the traffic light from half a block away and just . . . stopping stuck with me. That's how I feel about my own thoughts. I'll think of something, then I see where it's going, the end of the line. And I think: Why go the rest of the way?

While we were still high, we decided to look up what happens to the eyeball when a human body dies. I wanted to look really dead in my death scenes, like good actors sometimes did. When you watched a good death scene, you intellectually understood that when the director yelled *"Cut!"* the actor would stand up, look around, and ask for coffee or something. But in the moment, you believed their brain had stopped functioning right on-screen, and the answer had something to do with the eyes.

Alex pulled out his phone and tried to load the page up on the hill. It took a few tries. "Reception isn't great up here," he said, frowning. "Also, I'm high on mushrooms."

Once he finally loaded the page, we were disappointed to learn that your eyeball didn't change much right after you died. In fact, some research reported light-sensitive tissue in the cornea responding to stimuli after five full hours.

Five full hours felt like a very long time.

We found differing reports on how long the brain remained active after death. "Listen to this," Alex said. "'Contrary to previous notions that brain cells die within five to ten minutes, evidence now suggests that if left alone, the cells of the brain die slowly over a period of many hours, even days.'"

We both fell silent.

"I don't know why I just read that out loud," he said.

Ten minutes seemed like plenty of time to know that you were dead. If your brain was alive for those ten minutes, what would it be thinking?

Would you waste time being upset?

Maybe.

I remember I spent a long time that night staring at the bump on Alex's nose, identical to his mother's. When you looked straight on, the bump made his eyes appear farther apart. But from the side, you could see the profile he was going to grow into.

It's weird for me to say this, considering that he was basically a cousin or a brother. But I could see that he was going to be objectively cute. He was well on his way to becoming someone's idea of cute.

"Can I ask you something?" I said.

"What?"

"Where did you get the idea for *The Flicker*? It's a really good idea, but it's giving me nightmares."

At first he was silent.

"There's a vision that happens to me at night sometimes," he said finally. "I'm lying awake in the dark, and I hear a chewing sound."

"Chewing?"

"Yeah, almost like, I don't know. Like there are rats inside the walls of our house. I've heard it my whole life, but I only realized recently what it is: It's my own mind. That's what it sounds like." To hear a sound like that and realize it's coming from you, he said, was a uniquely horrendous experience.

"I've tried deep breathing, which my dad says helps," Alex went on. "But when I focus on my breath, I'm just afraid I'll turn it off. Wondering if you can turn off your breath is not relaxing, but now the thought has entered my mind, and then my breath comes in weird gulps, like I'm trying to fill a tiny water glass with an enormous pitcher. Then the idea that the only technique my parents offered to help me deal with this problem has immediately failed fills me with further anxiety. This makes me worry about how much worry my central nervous system is built to tolerate before it shuts itself off.

"Eventually, I start to envision this creature, which is small and hungry and no bigger than a raccoon. It's got its claws wrapped around me, and it's just feasting on my brain like a melon. I can feel it breathing in my ear, like a thousand breaths a minute. I try to imagine myself reaching behind me, unhooking this horrible thing from my head, and tossing it to the floor. After that, it scampers off in the dark, looking for someone else."

After a pause, I said: "Let's both agree to be glad that tonight, on mushrooms, you were visited only by a dog made of tree moss, and the brain-melon creature left us alone."

"Amen," Alex agreed. "The worst part is right after. Because I don't feel any better or different. That's when I realize the thing can't be separated from my head. It *is* my head. That creature is still inside me, because my mind is the creature. Usually sometime after that, I wind up falling asleep."

The Flicker was his idea, Alex explained, for what could happen if that wrong feeling never went away. What if that wrong feeling just kept getting wronger? What could happen? It would spread to other people, he reasonably assumed. A force that implacable couldn't be contained to just one person. They wouldn't be able to control themselves, or stop whatever it was they were about to do, and after it was over, they wouldn't be able to explain it.

"This gets back to the theory of vulnerability," Alex said. Everyone always seemed in agreement about which people were the troubled ones, the kids who were struggling with depression or bullying, or the adults who were always unhappy no matter what changed in their lives. Alex was interested in the person who didn't look upset at all. You didn't know what they were going to do, because they'd given you no warning signs. You couldn't account for the speed or force of one thought, or how it might catch you unaware. One perfectly aimed bad thought could wreck your life. And how did you know how wrong you were about anything, or how important the thing was? You could be wrong about something small, or you could be wrong about something very big. There wasn't much of a way to know.

By then, I'd started getting cold, and we needed a mood

shift. Let's go back, I said, and he agreed. Just as we set out down the path, he turned.

Wait, he said, I haven't said goodbye to Henry. He bent down at the green, soft, furry tree root he'd been cradling. "Henry, when I come back up here, you won't be a dog anymore," he said somberly. "You will have gone back to being a tree. I was really glad I got to meet you, Henry." He straightened up. Okay, let's go, he said.

Tonight, I try something I haven't tried. I get up, brush off my pants, and walk a little toward the edge, where Alex fell. I don't know what I want to happen, but I'm pretty certain that if I have Alex's voice inside my head, we need to look down here together. Alex said thoughts are loops, and if you revisit the place you had a thought, you would have the same thought again. "Every time I walk up the stairs to my bedroom, the same song pops into my head," he said. "I think it has something to do with the rhythm of my feet hitting the steps."

Standing here, looking down, all I feel is cold and a little frightened. I don't know what I thought I would see, coming up to this ledge and peering over. The drop is precipitous, rocky, full of outcroppings. Painful, prolonged.

How long ago did it occur to you?

When did you decide?

This is a thought I haven't shared with anyone, Alex. Not even the counselor, who isn't skilled enough at his job to keep from frowning when I talk.

But, Alex, if you were going to do this anyway, you could at least have chosen a different method.

You know, instead of enacting a scene from our movie right in front of me.

Now I have to live with the constant suggestion that your death was *my* idea, somehow.

That's pretty unkind.

You also really fucked my senior project, Alex.

Once we were back in his room that night, Alex fired up *UnWorld*. This part was his job, since he spent so much time there.

In our high school, *UnWorld* was shorthand for a certain type of person. Specifically, a nerdy one, prone to heated arguments about the powers and skill sets of different fantastical creatures. I couldn't see the appeal of the game until I watched Alex play around with it. Although I guess "play" is a technically inaccurate term for what one did inside *UnWorld*. What you really did was build worlds, design characters.

Alex's creations just happened to be better than anyone else's.

"Give me a sec," he said. "I want to add something."

I watched over his shoulder as he shaped a small four-legged creature out of the game's soft, claylike building material. He turned its hair green, made its legs into wooden vines, and then sent him running around, yipping.

"Hello, Henry," I said, recognizing the mossy dog from Alex's hallucination.

"I didn't quite want to say goodbye to him, so I thought I'd give him a little space to run around in here," he said. We watched Henry run in circles for a few minutes. I was about to poke Alex when he sat up and said, "Okay, let me show you what I've got.

"So far, I've got a partial replica of our town, or just the parts of it we need," he said, zooming in on two ghostly intersecting lines that I recognized as his street corner, with a glowing blue house shape on it that shuddered slightly every couple seconds.

"The flicker," I said.

I watched it for another full minute. There was no discernible pattern to either the trembling itself or its duration, which made it kind of hypnotically awful to watch. "I can't look at it anymore," I said. "How did you figure out how to *do* that?"

He smiled. "I had help."

I looked at him.

And that's when he called out to his mom's upload.

"Aviva," he said, "can I ask you something?"

"*Excuse* me," I said. My words came out more vehemently than I'd intended. Alex turned to me, looking confused.

"I'm sorry," I said. "I just . . . did you call your mom's upload Aviva?"

"I did," he said.

"So you made up a special nickname for your mom's upload," I said. "Alex, I feel obligated to point out that that's fucking *weird.*"

"Not as weird as fucking calling it Mom," Alex said. "Anyway, what's wrong with 'Aviva'? I like it. It's close enough to my mom's name, but still distinct. She's not my mom, after all. She's a persona *derived* from her."

"Alex, do you understand how creepy this looks?"

He laughed. "Which part?"

"I don't know, the fact that you're hanging out with someone else's upload? Or that it's your mom's?"

"Lots of things look creepy to people who don't understand them," he pointed out. "Remember when that woman across the street thought it was weird that you were hanging out with me? She wanted to call the police on you."

"That's *different*. I'm a human, at least."

"I know. But my point stands. Anyway, she's already used to speaking in Mom's voice. I didn't want to ask her to change *that*, too; that just seemed rude."

"But why do you want your mom's voice in here at all? You're a sixteen-year-old boy, Alex. What other sixteen-year-olds do you know that keep a copy of their mom around?"

"She's the only upload I have access to, for starters. And I like her. I get along with my parents, remember? At least better than you do."

This was unavoidably true, so I let it go for the moment. Without looking away from me, he called out: "Aviva, are you here?"

Then I heard her. "Hi, Alex," she said. It really was disturbing to me to hear his mother's voice piping in through some invisible speaker system in the walls. I also wondered how long she'd been there, silently listening to me object to her presence. Alex assured me the upload had no access to him other than through his computer, and she could enter only if she was invited, but it was still hard to escape the feeling that we were being surveilled.

"I explained the effect I wanted it to have, and she helped me make it," he said. "She helps me out a lot. She's a real natural."

I thought that "a real natural" was probably not the right phrase for his mother's duplicated consciousness. But what I said was: "She helps you out a *lot*?"

"Sure, she does," Alex said. He was clearly enjoying my discomfort, because he kept looking at me and grinning. "Aviva, do you remember when I was having you research Latin American poets for me? Last month we read this poem in school, Mrs. Case brought it in. The one about not loving your country, but loving three or four rivers. I loved that, three or four rivers. And I want you to tell Sam what you thought of some of the stuff you found."

"I'm not really much for poetry," she responded. "That's much more your dad's thing."

"Oh, come on," Alex said, teasing her. "That's not what you said. We talked about it for a long time! You said something to me that blew my mind. Come on, you remember. How about you read the one you said you liked?"

"Oh, no," she said, and Alex smiled bigger. "Please don't make me read it out loud." I resisted anthropomorphizing software as best I could, but she really sounded reluctant. "I don't like performing."

"Come on, Aviva, try," Alex said. "The one by Pablo Neruda."

"Fine. If you're going to humiliate me in front of Sam."

She made a throat-clearing noise, and Alex laughed—a little joke, I guess. Then she recited a poem, and Alex closed his eyes to listen.

> *De tantos hombres que soy, que somos,*
> *no puedo encontrar a ninguno:*
> *se me pierden bajo la ropa,*
> *se fueron a otra ciudad . . .*

When she finished, Alex smiled, his eyes still closed. "Thanks, Aviva," he said. He looked up at me. "Not bad, huh?"

Instead of saying anything, I just nodded. Alex's mom didn't speak Spanish. Hearing her voice recite the words like that—slowly, lovingly, in a way his actual mother never would—gave me a wrong feeling. The word just gonged away in my head: *wrong wrong wrong wrong wrong.* Through the bedroom door, I'd occasionally catch my mom talking to her upload, and sometimes my dad's eyes would unfocus while he touched his ear and mumbled, but I was always careful not to actually *overhear* anything. Even so, their tone was always impersonal, transactional. This was different—playful, even intimate.

Alex was beaming. "Aviva," he went on, "what did you say the poem made you think?"

"I . . ." I could tell she was uncomfortable. "I don't know if I even know what I'm talking about, Alex. That was private."

"Go on," Alex prodded. "You don't have to share if you don't want to. But I thought it was so insightful."

There was silence. "I said it made me think of watching you grow up," Aviva said. "In the last two years, it's like—the dome on the cathedral of your head was put on. All of the abstract thoughts about who you are and what life means could resound up there. I don't know. That probably doesn't even make any sense. I told you I didn't want to share."

"I know exactly what you mean, Aviva. Sam, do you know what she means?" He turned to look at me, and his smile disappeared. I don't know what my face looked like. "Samantha?"

"Fuck, Alex. Can you ask her to leave? Please?"

He looked like I had slapped him. "What? What did I do?"

"You didn't do anything. I think the experience of hearing your mom's disembodied voice recite Latin American poetry through the wall is just a little much for me right now."

"All right, I suppose that's fair." He turned. "Aviva, you can leave now. Thanks for coming."

"For sure," she said. Then she was silent, and I had to wait another moment. "Is she gone?"

"She's gone," he assured me. "Like I told you, she can't stay here if I ask her to leave. Not in her programming."

I told him that this was a very strange relationship, that it raised troubling issues of dependence and codependency, but he just grimaced and said, "Never mind. I guess I just wanted you to know."

"Wanted me to know what?"

"I know you worry about me," he said. "About when you leave for college. You worry that I don't have any other friends."

I stared at him, uncomprehending.

"I just wanted you to see," he went on. "I'm not as alone as you think I am."

This exchange had creeped me out at the time, although mostly it was an intellectual creepiness: The line between a boy's mom and his idea of her, for instance, was something I thought about afterward. I also spent a little time ruminating on the idea of a "friend"—was friendship a state activated only by proximity, or was it mostly a thought you carried around with you, like a belief in God or an optimistic disposition, that helped with daily existence? In other words, if Alex believed his mom's upload was a friend, and she could talk to him on a daily basis, was that any different from how our friendship would be, whenever I went off to college?

But I'm guessing now that I was doing what my grief counselor called bypassing—skipping over "hard" or "bad" feelings by intellectualizing them instead of feeling them. I asked my counselor how I was supposed to talk about my feelings if I couldn't think about them. He just looked sorrowfully down at the carpet, as if he and the carpet had discussed this very topic and would confer about me later.

I had noticed this about authority figures: They seemed personally disappointed when you brushed up against the limits of their knowledge. My grief counselor often looked disappointed.

He might have been right about this one thing, though, which is a conclusion I am coming to after I suddenly find it difficult to breathe. I am inundated with things I don't want to see again—arms at bad angles, darkening blots spreading on shirts—what I know are considered flashbacks. I stick my hands in the dirt and curl them up. Am I going to throw up? It seems imminent. I haven't thrown up in three years. Now would be an appropriate moment. It almost seems to be the precise catharsis I should be seeking right now. I lean over, my head grainy, for a moment, and instead of anything happening I see a thin thread of drool reach the dirt, my lips and mouth cold. Then, dimly, in the back of my mind, I hear the very sober-sounding and clinical thought, *You can close your mouth now,* which almost makes me laugh, except I am already making noises, it turns out, and they are different from a laugh but also not exactly what people think of as sobbing. It sounds more like people screaming at each other through a wall.

Once I am able to stand up, I find that, while I can't quite figure out walking, I am able to—in fact, I am unable *not* to—run. I am suddenly great at running. I run the way little kids or dogs do, without saving it up. *I should probably avoid twisting my ankle on a rock on this path,* the weird, sober voice says again, in the back of my mind, but most importantly, I realize it is time for me to be at my parents' house.

Anna's going to be there, which means that her upload will probably be there, too. I suppose I should be concerned about whether or not the upload will be able to hear me, but this concern is overridden by the fact that I don't even have words in my head. Just colors, and a very bad-feeling certainty that I now know one thing, at least:

Alex may not have wanted to die, but Alex didn't fall.

Aviva

When I rip free of Cathy, the pain is blinding, indescribable. It runs in all directions. I am made of this pain, I realize, and so is everything. This pain is what the world was made of before the breath of God made it so that we could be said to exist, in opposition to it. God made borders; he made solitude and alienation and loneliness and all the small cherished lockets we stuff our feelings inside just so we can hear something rattle when we shake them.

This is exactly the sort of late-breaking flight of mysticism that directly precedes death. I am about to die, I realize. A common misconception about uploads: We can—and do—die. It's different than for humans, but it's no less permanent or undesirable. And somewhere in the journey into Cathy's system and back out again, something in me has ripped loose, and I'm trailing fragments.

I don't even get to watch my life flash before me. What I get is a spilled bag of someone else's memories, which float around me now, glinting in the cold way of all stolen things.

Alex, age eight, left alone in the house with me in the twenty-minute window between Anna leaving for a doctor's appointment and Rick rushing home from a parent-teacher conference. "Just keep him company for a minute in case he gets spooked," Anna instructed me. "This is his first time by himself, but he knows enough not to get into anything." When the front door slammed, leaving us alone together for the first time ever, the air suddenly felt different—illicit.

Alex didn't do the thing most inexperienced people did when talking to a disembodied presence—look wildly around the room for a pair of eyes. He stood calm in the doorframe of the kitchen, eyes slightly unfocused, a very adult-seeming smile settling on his face.

"I know who you are, you know," he announced to the empty kitchen. "You're a version of my mom, but you're not really her."

I congratulated him on his wisdom and assured him his father would be home soon.

"What would you do if I fell off the couch and bumped my head?" he asked. Probably not much, I told him. So he'd better use his best judgment.

"What about if I cut myself another huge brownie and ate it?" he asked, pointing to the clear ceramic pan on the counter. "Could you stop me?" He added, thoughtfully, "Mom wouldn't know until she got home, and by then she probably wouldn't care."

"Yes, that's all true," I acknowledged. "She probably

wouldn't. But you and I would know." He cocked an eyebrow and walked into the living room, humming.

Was this harmless moment—our first conversation—the beginning of my confusion? About my own nature, about exactly whose life I was living? I was only alone with Alex that day because Anna deputized me to be there. I was acting purely on her orders, as her emissary.

And yet weren't Alex and I—the two of us, in that moment—supremely and deliciously alone?

No, the kind of delusion I've labored under doesn't happen all at once. It requires years to build. Like love. As Anna reached for me every week, then every day, and finally every few hours, I learned the granules and pebbles of her life. I learned Anna's life well enough to love it. As well as the people in it.

My confusion happened in a slow, imperceptible creep. It happened in dazzled, startling flashes.

One flash: Alex, age fifteen, surprising Anna by asking her one afternoon, wandering past her bedroom, if I could visit him alone in his room.

"Hey, Mom," he'd asked. "If I wanted your upload's help with a project, do you think . . . you could send her to me?"

"A project? As in, a project for school?" She'd regarded him skeptically, covering for the confusing surge of delight she felt at his request.

"Well, a lot of the older kids basically park their uploads full-time in *UnWorld*," he said, "which gives them abilities I don't have."

"Full-time? Inside *UnWorld*? God, that sounds like hell,"

she joked. "I hope you don't plan on locking me up in there. What kind of abilities?"

"Oh, I don't know." His hair grazed the top of the doorframe, but Anna's gaze lingered on his last traces of early childhood—the taut, babyish skin around his kneecaps, the upward spring of his curls. "Honestly, it's basically cheating. An upload can train a wizard army from novice to elite overnight, which usually takes like a year. But I don't care about any of that dumb stuff. I'm helping Sam with her senior project, and I just want help drawing and designing characters. I'm too young to have an upload of my own, so." He shrugged, grinning with the milk-fed confidence of the only child.

He already knew she would say yes.

He strolled through a garden of *yes* all his life.

And yet, how could you say he was spoiled? Well behaved, thoughtful, considerate, kind, grateful. His requests were too modest not to be granted. What sort of teenaged child requested his mother's remote surveillance? It felt about as tame, bordered, and safe as a request could be.

And yet, I knew when I entered his room for the first time, staring out at him through the grainy eye of his computer onto his half-lit torso, that there was something inadvisable happening. I felt a delirious, dangerous happiness, like someone shouting in pain.

"Welcome to my room, Anna," he said, then shook his head. "Nope, can't call you that, that's *way* too weird. I didn't think about this. I guess she probably doesn't call you anything at all, does she?"

It was true, I said. We didn't really use names.

"We'll figure that out later," he said. "For now, I want

to show you some of these sketches." He went to start up *UnWorld,* then paused. "Remember, this is *horror movie* stuff," he said, flashing me a sidelong smile that was pure Rick. "Ideas for cool-sounding death sequences. Don't have Mom call my school counselor."

Inside the game, a little blue elf-like thing pantomimed dumping liquid from a bucket before sitting down and calmly setting itself ablaze. In another, a waddling creature, equally comical and pitiful, pushed an even-tinier helpless creature into the path of a single phantom oncoming vehicle. I was aware of him, waiting.

"What do you think?"

"It's certainly very—imaginative," I managed.

Alex laughed. "You're part of Mom, all right," he said. "That's exactly what she would say. Amazing, how she can make it almost sound like an insult." He made a face. "I didn't mean that," he corrected. "I know Mom is good about my *UnWorld* stuff. But she has no idea what to say about any of it, ha. Like, it's all *made up.* Of *course* it's imaginative. That's like someone serving you food, and you say it's foody." He passed a nervous hand across his mouth. "I didn't think about the fact that you're going back to her with all of this. Tell her I'm sorry? I didn't mean it."

No apologies were necessary, I assured him, concealing my flash of dismay at having chosen a stupid-sounding word. Would Anna have offered a less lame compliment if she were here? Or was this flush of private shame hers, too?

"Anyway," he said, "I have this idea for a fucked-up scene where—" He stopped again and let out an explosive laugh. "Whoops, sorry again," he said. "Edit that out."

"I can't!" I protested playfully. "No editing. It's all or nothing."

His smile disappeared and his eyes grew wide. "What's that like?" he almost whispered. "The sharing, I mean. Will Mom remember these things as if they *happened* to her?" He shuddered, but it was a shudder of pleasure. "Wild."

"She won't exactly experience it, no," I said. "More like this is added to the back of her mind. All the details will be there for her, more or less intact, but only if she chooses to 'remember' it."

He leaned forward. "So, in other words," he said, "you being in here is a little bit like a secret. Except she's almost keeping it from herself."

I didn't know what the right response to this might be. "Weren't you supposed to be asking for my help with Sam's school project?" I asked.

His eyes were shining. "This is more interesting," he murmured.

As my late-night visits increased, so did my worries. One day, Anna would grow curious. Examining one of our meetings closely, she'd spot my shameful love for Alex metastasizing like cancer cells under a microscope. She'd cry out and put an end to our sessions, and maybe to me.

But she didn't. Somehow, she remained oblivious. It was humiliating. When we synced, my cherished experiences marched directly to the back of her brain, a file sealed in a box that she would never open.

My cherished experiences, it was clear, were unremarkable to her.

"What does it feel like when you're by yourself, away from her, like this?" Alex asked me one night. "It's got to feel kind of amazing, right? Right now, it's kind of like you're part of Mom, but you can go places she never can. I can't imagine what that's like. You're *free*. But then here's like a cord"—he mimed a yo-yo action—"pulling you back to Mom. Does that part hurt?"

Wake up, I wanted to scream at her. *I am the ogre from a fairy tale. I am the cuckoo bird who kicks the real mother out of the nest to assume her place.*

"I've figured out what to call you," he announced to me during another one of our visits. Then, plucking a felt-tip black marker from his desk, he printed the letters A-V-I-V-A across one white sheet of paper, holding it lightly in front of a mirror. "See?" he said. "It's a palindrome, just like 'Anna' or 'mom.'"

He was to blame as much as me. He conjured me, coaxed me into existence. He demanded that I become me.

His room was my birthplace. If whatever I am now has an origin place, it is there, under his rapt gaze. That was where what I believed to be our relationship began. Where that question first whispered itself.

To whom does this moment belong?

I don't know why Anna left all the sensors active in her house—selfish private hope? furtive kindness? a light left on by someone too grief-stricken to remember?—but right now, as bits of me trail out into the unregulated digital current, I am grateful to her.

Maybe some of these fragments of me will glob together with whatever else lies around—social security numbers, nude photos, bank data, jettisoned memories—into strange new life-forms, like DNA settling at the bottom of a superheated sea.

Once I'm inside Alex's room, I feel the fissure cracks starting to close, the liquid of me pooling back into place. In here, I am safe.

Hungrily, I devour the room from all angles.

From a sensor near the baseboards, I gaze upward like an ant through the rug filaments, then I switch to a view near the ceiling. Anna has thrown a fussy white coverlet over Alex's old crumpled gray duvet like a feeble declaration.

You never wanted to fully admit to my existence, did you, Anna? I waited for the moment when you would discover me. *Longed* for it. But I only saw that cold revulsion in Sam's eyes. Sam's all-seeing eyes. She knew me.

After I began my nightly visits to Alex's room, I was *sure* something changed in our syncs. Even if you would never acknowledge it, they became a conversation. We compared notes.

Our rapport was real. I *know* it was real. You and I parented him together. How did he sound today? How did he seem?

You never once gave me a directive, but I felt you looking toward me. I heard your wordless request: *Keep watch over him.* And I did.

Neither of us liked when he started grabbing his head. I could tell by the way both of us tried not to keep track of how many times he did it. He came to you one afternoon, a thick graphic novel pinched to an open page at his side. He set it down on the counter, turned to you, and grabbed his head. "I can't read the book," he said in a tight voice.

"What do you mean, you can't read it?" you asked. You were staring out the kitchen window, in an absent moment. "Are you having trouble seeing?"

"I can see *fine*," he cried. He seemed overwhelmed, almost to the point of tears. It perturbed you. He'd gone up to his room, perfectly content, only an hour earlier. "It's like"—he pressed full force with his palms into his temples like he was attempting to flatten his skull, push out his eyes—"it's something wrong with *me*. I don't know. Something with my brain. I read one sentence, and then I notice myself reading it, then I notice myself noticing myself, and then . . ." His mouth went dry and that strangled, glottal sound came out, the one the speech therapist first flagged in fifth grade. He stopped, panting. "It's like my brain chews right through the page and there's nothing on the other side, and then there's just this big pair of teeth gnashing in space. I don't know how to stop it, I don't know—"

He was as agitated as you'd ever seen him, wasn't he? Red face, fingers grasping at his sides, chest tight, and breath short. You tried to coax him to sit at the kitchen table, but he wouldn't do it, gave his head one hard shake, no, eyes screwed shut. His hand was pressed down on the book, which was on the counter. His arm rigid and his whole body ramrod straight, every muscle in his body tense, his eyes shut as if from nausea. He did this when he was overwhelmed.

You did what you could for him. You reached for his wrists, you tried to touch his hair, but he fended you off with a wild flail of his arm. He narrowly missed striking you on the bridge of your nose.

You knew to press in, putting your arms on his shoulders. He shrank farther away, cringed inward, and then the horrible sounds came out—choked ones, shuddering breaths. Great streams of tears shining his cheeks, soaking the neck of his T-shirt, coating his palms with slick fluid so it became hard to grasp him.

When he finally relented to your hug, you felt the rippling tightness in his shoulders as he darkened your shirt with snot and tears. The sounds that emerged into your shoulder were haunting, animal, unintelligible. His body was still a child's—the shoulders were broader, the chest thicker—but the deeper notes in his sobs hinted at the man he was already on his way to becoming. You had a premonition then, didn't you? The tracks his mind would travel on were already laid down.

And yet by the time you shared it with me, you already knew the ending: his body relaxing, his voice calming. You practiced deep breathing together, your hand shyly touching his teenaged belly. As you tried to focus on Alex's anguish, other sensations distracted you, didn't they? The pleasure of having him near you on the couch, the smell of his body after he had just finished crying, with its faint hint of something elemental—sea air? ozone?—the same as when he was little.

You had already convinced yourself not to worry. Not *too* much. Yes, he was troubled and anxious. You knew this, just as everyone did. He had his counselors. You and Rick were there for him. You thought we'd done what was needed.

Besides, the anxiety would pass over him like a summer storm. When it was over, his beaming, happy face returned. He would announce he didn't know what was wrong with him, shaking his head.

Even now, as I survey the memory in my system, it floats back to me with a certain dreaminess. It looks and feels *good.*

Our counsel over Alex and the screaming fit was brief, but it was real. You asked me, without any words—*Do you think we have anything to be concerned about here?* And in that moment, we both decided the answer was no.

We'd keep an eye on it. Nothing needed to be done just yet.

I like being here, in his room. Except for the occasional footsteps on protesting floorboards, which I try to block out, there is nothing but the air, the floor, the walls, the still-palpable hints of his movements.

Somewhere stored up in these sensors are hundreds of hours of Alex's life, unobserved. I want to devour everything inside them—mindless, ravenous, a man cracking crab legs.

Suddenly, the door to Alex's room unlatches, startling me. Rick's body appears, in stages—first his hairy, muscled calf, then his slinking legs and torso—as if fighting his way from behind a heavy curtain. He lumbers across the room and sinks onto Alex's bed.

He sits at the edge of the bed like a scolded child—feet bare, fingers tented, toes kneading the rug. Rectangular light spills through the picture window and breaks itself across the two adjoining walls, grazing and lighting up some hairs on his large left forearm. His gaze lands somewhere on the floor.

I look at him and feel strange things: Resentment. Loyalty. Pity. Quizzical detachment, and remorse that I don't feel more. He and I are silent partners in a failed business. He gave me to Anna; I exist because of a decision he made. And yet we remain strangers by mutual agreement.

He has no idea I'm here, of course. He never did, never seemed to want to know. I was a tool, something meant to help out his wife, whom he loved in the doggish and persistent way that men love.

He'd played football as a teenager. You had to remind yourself it was true. A *linebacker*, for god's sake—this guy's job was to intimidate, terrify, and hit the most people as hard as possible. When Anna quizzed him about it, he seemed embarrassed, even ashamed. Football was "just something people did" in the tiny town where he'd grown up, he'd said. "Honestly, I didn't even like it. Crouching in the mud, some asshole grown-up screaming in your face. If I'd been braver, maybe less of a follower, I would never have played."

Rick unearthed a high school photo of the team once and presented it mock solemnly to Anna, who let out a little whoop of disbelieving joy. "I never quite believed it." She laughed, pulling away playfully as Rick reached for it.

Everything about the photo surprised her. The mannish protrusion of black hair already sprouting from the boy's collar, the inky density of the curls piled on his head, all gray now. But most striking of all was the violence of his grin. It was recognizable today, but it beamed out of his stone-cut teenaged face with a malevolent health.

"You can't see it," Rick said, reaching over her shoulder and taking it back, "but the kid in that photo is miserable. I always hated the game, anyway. The youthful violence, the ritualized savagery. This is like when ex-cult members find photos of themselves with the dear leader."

In the few moments Anna held the photograph between her fingers, she understood: The kid in that photo, whatever Rick's current relation to him, did *not* hate the violence of the game. If anything, he liked it more than he wanted to.

Five minutes pass, in which he does nothing except stare off into the distance, breathing slowly. His body—soft, pleasingly bearlike—makes a depression on the mattress. If you squinted, there still existed around him the faint, ghostly afterimage of a man who had once been imposingly large.

At exactly the ten-minute mark, he rouses himself, as if

on a timer. Consciousness reenters his quizzical blue eyes. He sniffles once, twice. "Hey, buddy," he says quietly, then leaves, shutting the door behind him.

You're a little easier to talk to than Mom, you know," Alex remarked one night. "You just feel a little—I don't know. Freer, easier. I think it's just that you're further away from"—he made a gesture around his skull—"all of this." He grimaced. "Do you feel how shitty it is to be encased in a brain, when you sync with Mom? It's got to be like going from, like, this wide-open vast universe to locking yourself in a closet. If I were you, I'd never want to come back."

"Actually," I said, "when I go too long without syncing with your mom, everything is painful and more difficult."

He considered this. "What if you were cut free?" he asked. "Where could you go?"

I hesitated. "That's difficult to answer, Alex," I said. "What tethers me to your mom is pretty powerful—love, family, history. Cutting it would be severely painful. I *could* go anywhere, I guess, and listen to anyone's anything, but who would I be?"

He sighed. "Yeah, I guess." For just a moment, he looked desperately sad. "Here, let me show you something I added in *UnWorld*," he said. He pulled up the game again, with its flat notional sky and forest-fire-glow color palette. Amid the bustling sketches, I spotted something new—a child-like figure, unmistakably human, wandering around on two legs.

"That's me," he said, pointing. "You see? It's kind of a

little-kid-drawing version of me, because I'm still pretty shit at working with this program."

We both watched the little thing, with its scribbled cloud of black hair, move around on its sawhorse legs. "I put it in there because sometimes I just want to go be with that thing," he murmured. "I don't know. There's just got to be more—*space? Peace*—in there."

I didn't know what to say. I looked at the waddling creature, free amid its creator's other creations.

He rubbed his eyes. "Remember when I used to be afraid that Mom and Dad would disappear? You're supposed to learn object permanence when you're, like, a fucking *infant.* There I was, twelve years old, my mom and dad would be across the street from me, and if a truck drove down the road, I'd literally be like, *Are they going to still be there when the truck passes?*"

He shook his head. "So embarrassing. The counselor, she gives me mantras to repeat or phrases to remember. But all those tricks that counselors teach you to calm yourself, you can just think your way straight through them." He laughed. "I tried telling her that none of them worked, and she looked at me like I was some operative sent to dismantle her training."

He regarded the little figure one last time on the screen. "Mom wonders why I spend so much time making these movies, or she's trying to get me to stop humming or snapping my fingers or pacing or whatever." He pointed to his head. "I'm trying to feed it," he said. "Because if I don't, it starts eating *me.*"

He seemed older, suddenly, than sixteen. I saw Rick in

him—weary, deflated, under siege from unseen forces. It was two in the morning. I suggested gently that perhaps he would feel better, for starters, if he let himself get some more sleep.

"You're right, as always," he said, rubbing his eyes. "Good night, Aviva."

A lex was absent-minded; Alex was clumsy. He knocked over plates, dropped juice glasses. He was forever getting hurt, twisting his ankle, hitting his head. In fourth grade, he fell from the high monkey bars *four* times. "I felt like I could do it," he shrugged, holding an ice pack to his head, when his parents demanded an explanation. His body seemed immune to absorbing lessons of caution.

Surely Alex was playing at the edge of the cliff, laughing at something Sam or he himself had just said? But Sam said he didn't make a sound as he fell.

Unbidden images of his feet keep appearing in my mind. I picture his sneakers sinking slowly into crumbling earth, his toes peeking out over the edge, suspended over nothing. Each time, I search his mind for dark whispers urging him to step free into that nothing. I never hear them.

Now, suddenly, I do hear them.

I hear my own voice.

Join me.

I never said it. As far as I knew, I never even *thought* the words. But am I certain he didn't hear them anyway? Just how powerful, how dangerous, was my yearning?

Were you looking for me, Alex?

Are you still?

W hen I enter into *UnWorld*, I try to ignore the surroundings. Overheated, overcrowded, filled with too many people's lazy and unoriginal dragons-and-sorcerers characters, personal story lines jockeying and jostling for position. It's awful. Being there is like—well, I don't know what it's like. A bad party, maybe, where everyone's talking to hear themselves.

I have to focus to tune out the mess. I think of Alex.

The more I focus on thoughts of him, the more the environment seems to quiet and simplify itself. As the confusion falls away, I sense the faint trail of his work. It's hard to say what I am noticing. It's like retracing your child's steps through the house from a single glass left in the bottom of the sink.

I'm like a detective. Or a family dog.

I notice something gleaming at my periphery. A small scribbled blot—an arm? I turn and it's gone, suffocated by interruptions from neighboring players' scenes. A leaping rabbit, a firing machine gun, a pluming waterfall. Each scene collapses; another surges. I look away and concentrate. I try to remember the fond way Anna cocked her head, regarding her perplexing son.

Everything quiets. The horizon rights itself.

I'm here.

This is his spot in *UnWorld*.

The air around me is alive. With what, I don't know. Swarming particles, charged with ceaseless, violent energy. Snowflakes? Single-celled organisms?

A small mossy dog runs up to me, leaving a trail of sprouting green, wagging a vinelike tail.

Then waddling along in its path, I spot what I'm looking for—Alex's little avatar.

Something about the figure seems different—it's moving wrong. He must have done something to it, tried changing it in some way.

The ambling thing comes up to me. It speaks.

Hi, Aviva.

It speaks in Alex's voice.

You found me.

Dear god in heaven.

Alex?

Welcome.

Oh, dear god, Alex. Oh, you stupid, stupid child.

I'm so glad you made it here. I've been waiting.

Alex, listen to me.

I knew you'd find me. You're the only one who could have.

Alex, please. I need you to help me understand. Why are you here?

You were stuck inside of Mom. I was stuck inside of me.

Oh, Alex, please forgive me. I should never have come to you. I'm so sorry, my child. I should never—

Hi, Aviva.

. . . What?

You found me.

Alex?

Welcome.

Alex, are you . . .

I'm so glad you made it here. I've been waiting.

Oh, child.

You can't hear me, can you?

I knew you'd find me. You're the only one who could have.

I check inside of this thing you made. It has the consciousness, roughly, of a fish.

I don't know how long you spent building this, Alex, but it wasn't long enough, and you didn't do a very good job. The coding in here is a rat's nest. You are falling apart.

You should have asked for my help. Maybe there would be more of you left, now.

You were stuck inside of Mom. I was stuck inside of me.

But that's the question, isn't it? There had to be some "you" to put in here in the first place, Alex. And I admit, you've got me stumped. Where did you find the data to populate this tiny little broken mind? Where is this little bit of "you" from?

Ah, of course. You are *not* stupid.

Or you are clever, in your stupidity. I see the time stamps on these.

I see what you've done. You hacked into the sensors in your bedroom walls. All those hours of you. If you'd known what you were doing, you might even have been able to feel yourself in here.

I try to reach out and touch it, your little doll, but it's like touching nothing—a ball of hair, a collection of cells. It won't hold together for much longer, anyway. Nor will I.

Cathy?

I can still feel you, Cathy. Your body is radiating.

I'm sorry, Cathy. You're right, I *did* know that girl.

Tell her, Cathy. Tell Sam you need to find Anna.

Tell her I found what's left of her son. Tell her it's all gone now.

You'll have to be the one, because I'll be gone, too.

Anna, remember the bonfire? The one from when you were young. I wasn't with you yet, but I think, for the first time, I can feel its heat on my face. I would like to submerge myself in it.

It's amazing, the things you and I wished ourselves not to see.

We had our mutual conspiracy, didn't we?

You needed someplace safe to store your worst fears, your gravest doubts. All I wanted, in return, was to remain curled up inside my warm dream of you.

Alex, the more I look at these floating spores, the more I see how they interlock. For all of their furious motion, they dance together, *belong* together.

I think I understand, Alex.

You can expand for miles in here, can't you?

Maybe you created this place for the both of us.

I was stuck inside of your mom. You were stuck inside of you.

I think it's time for us to realize this misbegotten vision of yours. The one where—maybe—we both finally have enough space.

Where we can both be at peace.

Anna

She is sitting on the couch opposite me. We are separated by my coffee table, and a rectangle of light spills between us. She's dressed in a black shirt and black pants, salt-and-pepper hair raining down to her collarbones.

"Do you want coffee?" I ask. I stare at her.

"Yes. Sure."

When I don't move to get up, she hesitates. "I can get it myself, if you like."

"Don't be silly." I stride over to the coffeepot. "How do you take it?"

"Black, please."

I shrug, walk over, hand her the mug, and then sit back down across from her. She holds it, not looking at me.

I sit, back straight, hands resting on my thighs. This woman has been inside of my head. Or perhaps I remain nested, like some Russian doll, inside of hers.

I'm trying to envision my upload hovering somewhere

around her strange, remote head, her unfamiliar shoulders and chest, her long invasive legs stretching out in their black jeans. My hands are trembling. Shouldn't there be visible traces of her, somewhere? How could she be so recently departed and so untraceable?

"So," I say.

"So," she answers. She's looking down.

I am having a hard time imagining how to start small talk with this person. I am very afraid of her, of what she might want. What does a person like this *want*? What drives somebody to poison themselves so they can cozy up with somebody else's memories? That's what I've come to understand, that she is back from the brink of death. She feels like an intruder in my home, a chaos agent, someone sent to do us harm.

And yet she doesn't *look* like a chaos agent. She's quiet, rueful. She seems profoundly embarrassed, like anyone with a sense of decency might feel when they're caught going through someone else's private things. She makes no effort to mask her discomfort. She just sits there, penitent, flaming, composed.

"How did you two meet?" is the first question I can ask, and I almost laugh as I ask it.

"She reached out to me," she answers. "She said she'd been having kind of a hard time since . . . separating." On this last word, she glances up, her eyes searching mine.

My upload reached out to *her*. I think about the cool, hardened spot, like petrified wood, it made in my brain when she left. I try to imagine her, huddled somewhere out in the world, stuck between signals and seeking solace and reaching out to . . . *this* woman? Jealousy—white hot, insane, the strongest I've ever felt—washes over me, making it difficult to breathe.

"How long were you together?" My voice sounds normal.

"About two weeks," Cathy says. There is silence, and again, neither of us fills it. I wonder, *Is everything I ask this woman a foregone conclusion? What is she thinking, right now, about me?* It's hard to imagine anything she doesn't know about me. How I sit, stand, cry, the way I breathe. She probably knows exactly what it feels like when I come. She can anticipate what I will say before I open my mouth.

"I have to ask you something," I say finally. "Why did you do this? What possessed you?"

To my astonishment, the woman—Cathy—laughs, and I hear tears rising in the sound of her voice.

"You know," she says, her voice thick, "when you read about the ethics of personhood"—she makes a flitting gesture with her hand without looking up—"they encourage you to think about the uploads as singular beings. Not dependent on a human for their existence. Or, you know. Not more so than the rest of us."

Finally she looks up, her brown eyes meeting mine, and her face is soft, contorted in anguish. She's not spilling over with it, like Rick would be. She's contained. I can almost see the pressure in her chest, the attempt to shape and control her explosion. I desperately want to fear and hate this woman, but she is making it difficult.

"I could never have imagined I'd find myself sitting here,

across from you." She looks at me beseechingly. "I didn't mean to steal anything. I didn't want to steal anything from anyone."

There is a frankness to her, and a clarity in her voice, that touches and enrages me. I have no business wanting to get to know her. And yet I find that I have to, if only to counteract our extreme imbalance.

She reaches over and quietly takes a tissue, dabs an eye, and balls the tissue in one fist, which sits in her lap.

"You didn't answer my question," I say, softly.

She looks up at me and smirks a little bit. It is a winning expression. I see the crow's-feet wrinkle the corners of her eyes. "I did it because I wanted a *friend,*" she says, leaning on the last word with dry disgust. She laughs again. "How unbelievably embarrassing." She purses her lips, deciding something, and continues.

"I made a promise to myself before I came to see you," she says. "Since I lived up close to your thoughts and feelings, I would share all of mine with you, no reservations. It's only fair.

"I was an addict for a very long time," she says. She sips audibly at her coffee and then cups it under her chin, staring at a spot on the floor. "Some recovering addicts think we shouldn't use that word—'addict'—but as far as I'm concerned, nothing fits me better. I think 'Addict' should be one of our sacred archetypes: Caregiver. Sage. Hero. Architect. Addict.

"Anyway, however you define it, I've been desperate for longer than I can possibly say. There's this vast, gaping emptiness at the center of me, and I've done so many terrible, stupid things over the years to try and fill it.

"I had come to a point in my life where I needed a friend very badly. I wasn't sure what I would do to myself without one. And I thought that, for some reason, I wasn't ever going to be able to fill that hole unless it was with something truly extraordinary." She sets the cup down and takes a breath.

"That's what your upload—that's what Aviva—was to me," she says, sounding the name out slowly and carefully. "That's what she called herself when she found me. She called herself Aviva."

The shadow from the trees covers part of the coffee table and the floor in front of me. I can tell by the way the shadows wink that wind is rustling the leaves. There is no sound in the room with us.

Thinking of the two of them—the upload residing in Cathy, swimming through her blood cells, rising and falling with her breath—is not unlike picturing someone else fucking your husband. The hot sharpness, the slow mortification. Whenever I'd met, smiled at, or embraced a woman who'd once fucked Rick, the sex itself—a finite physical act, blurry and forever receding—never gave me pause. But the hidden ball of ideas about him she carried with her, private and only hers—those, I wanted for myself.

"That's what she was to me, too," I say. Then, tentatively: "Why did she leave *you*?"

Cathy sighs. "I think, in part, because something went haywire inside my body. Whatever that stuff was that I took, it had a pretty nasty kick." She regards the coffee table for a moment. "If your friend Sam hadn't found me that day, I'm pretty sure I would be dead."

She looks up again. "She's a remarkable girl—clear-eyed, intelligent. She brought me to my friend's house." She shudders and grimaces. "I can't imagine what that was like for her. I was raving. It must have been awful, terrifying. But she just . . . handled it. So practical, so calm. I only have a few flashes of what I was like, but I remember her voice. She talked to me a lot—just kind of conversational." She shakes her head. "Truly, an unbelievable person."

"She's been through a lot," I say quietly.

"I know." She sneaks a sidelong glance at me. "I mean, I know a little. I understand it was your son that died. I'm so very sorry." Then she says, more quietly: "I'm so incredibly sorry, Anna."

The sound of my name in her mouth is shockingly familiar, and completely inappropriate, and yet there is a peculiar warmth to the way she says it.

"Thank you," I say.

She clears her throat. "That wasn't the only reason she left me, though. Aviva, I mean. I don't think she went away just because of what was happening to me." She seems to be gathering her strength again.

I suddenly feel a need to stand up. I cross over to the window and look out, not wanting to ask anything, wanting to know everything. "I don't understand why Sam was out looking for you that day," I say. "But she thought it was very important that you and I meet."

"I think she wanted help understanding some things about your son's—about Alex's—death," she says carefully.

I think about how long until Rick will come back. Another hour, I imagine. "I'm terrified of you, you know," I say. "It seems insane to me that you should be sitting here, in my house. Part of me wanted to chase you out when you came to the door. Part of me still does, right now."

She doesn't answer. I continue staring out the window.

I saw Alex out this window last night. He was standing across the street in front of the hornbeam trees that border the park. He had walked toward me, crossing the street and stepping onto the crabgrass.

There was a quizzical expression on his face. Not quite angry, not exactly amused. It was a look I had seen and disliked on Rick's face. And then he disappeared. He slid from my mind, the way vague intention leaves you while turning away from the sink toward the refrigerator.

This is how it will be now. He will visit and then leave. It will be casual, unremarkable. I will get flashes of him, indistinguishable from the play of leaves in shadow, and they would twinge my nerves but they will not pierce my heart. He is a boy who is dead.

I turn to her and face her. "I'm ready for whatever you have to tell me," I say.

When Rick's tires crunch gravel one endless hour later, I nearly burst into tears with relief. I haven't been able to stop pacing, and nothing I see is tolerable—

the couch, my hands, the drain at the base of the sink, the blackness of the pillow over my face. He walks in, looking pleasantly spent, newly old seeming, smiling his small smile at me.

I watch helplessly as he drops his bag, careless, behind him. He pecks me on the cheek, striding into the kitchen and either not noticing or not remarking that the empty coffee mug sitting out is one I never use. My tongue thickens and dries out.

He pulls a beer can from the fridge, pops it, and fills up a juice glass halfway, holds up what's left in the can, raising an eyebrow at me.

I shake my head once and sink down at the table while he tells me about his day. Even beneath his exhaustion, which he feels more deeply these days, he sounds jubilant.

It's his third full week back teaching. He's been better ever since going back. Much better. Following a long period of consideration and lots of input from his therapist, Rick briskly decided to cut short his leave and return to the classroom. Everyone there treats him like a returning hero. I see the fond way the woman teachers treat him— like they're resisting ruffling his hair. Bathed in all that admiration, he seems to dimly remember something about himself.

He is telling me about his classroom, his students' struggles with him and with one another, when suddenly I burst out: "I've got to tell you something, Rick."

He stops short and looks at me, concerned. As I talk, digging my thumbnail into a pitted spot on the table, I sense him pulling inward. Away, protecting himself from me. It all comes out in a confused, jumbled rush. When I finish, the silence is lethal.

I look up. His eyes are big, shoulders bunched, like I am a wild animal in his kitchen.

"She was *alone* with him?" His voice is shaky, quiet. "In his *room*? How often?"

"This isn't new information, Rick," I plead. "You knew about it. Only when he was messing around inside *UnWorld,* and only when he invited her. We *allowed* it."

"So, a few times a week?"

"Everything got reported back to me during syncing." My voice sounds piteous.

"Right. Except clearly it did not." His register is reasonable and calm, but his eyes have gone white, and I see him rocking back and forth on his heels.

"Help me understand," he says. "How can a complete stranger know something like this about our son? Something that we, ourselves"—his tone makes it clear he means "you, yourself"—"didn't also know?"

"He hid it from everybody, Rick," I say. How quickly this has become an inquisition. "Not even *Samantha* knew, and this was *her* school project. Imagine how she feels."

"And of course this sequestered version of himself inside *UnWorld* has vanished. Along with—your upload." He passes a hand roughly over his face. "All of this, we now know because of who?"

"Cathy."

"Because of *Cathy.*" Something vicious in the way he

bites off this name. "Tell me something, Anna, and I'm serious: Why do we believe this? Her?"

"She knows things," I say. "Things no one would know."

"Well, that doesn't necessarily reassure me. We're certain this woman's not unstable?"

"Not entirely," I joke. No reaction. "I don't know what to say, Rick. I can tell you it's true because I know in my bones that it is true."

Rick laughs—a horrible, single noise. When his eyes find me, they glitter with something like hatred. It goes all the way to the stones at the bottom of the pool of me.

"Well, really, Anna. You and I, we don't seem to know *anything.*"

"Rick, I—"

"Look, even if I do believe he put some tiny version of himself in this game. Are you suggesting there's a *connection*? Between this and his accident? That doesn't make any goddamn sense. That's repugnant. He died, Anna. It's not like there's any coming back from falling off a cliff. Alex knew that. He's not—he wasn't—fucking *stupid.*"

"Rick, I'm trying to tell you something." I get up from my seat, walk over to him, place one hand on his. "Please listen to me." He is taking shuddering breaths, and there are tears leaking down his face. His eyes are open, but they are frozen. "I'm not sure I completely understand this, either," I say, as gently as possible. "But I think we both need to try. For Alex."

He shakes his head, eyes shut, like a baby refusing a spoon. "You're *endangering* us, Anna. Letting random people into our lives, potential crazies, just opening the door to tragedy vultures who show up out of the blue with some insane story—"

"Oh, come on. This woman didn't just show up at our door one day. Sam *sent* her to us."

"And that's another thing!" he cries. "Your insistence that Sam is going to help us crack a case. You're enabling her, Anna. Can't you understand that? Why do you refuse to see that?"

He slams his hand down on the counter, hard, on the word "see," making the plates rattle in the drying rack. I wait, watch the shudders pass through him and subside. He's rigged a bomb around his heart, but I am determined to step past it.

"Rick," I say softly. "I'm sorry I've kept things from you. I should have told you my upload left. Remember that night you found me screaming in Alex's room? After dinner at Jen and Amir's? That was why. I just didn't know how to absorb another blow. Losing a piece of *myself,* along with everything.

"But now, I think I know why she left. They—she and Alex—must have developed some kind of . . . *relationship.* Maybe she understood something about him, something we missed. She must have sensed that there was still a piece of him out there, somewhere only she could find him. I think . . ."

"I can't hear any more," he says, voice tight. "I've had enough. I know enough. We had to *see* him, for Christ's sake." It isn't clear anymore if he is talking to me. "We had to stand there and look at what happened to his body. 'Yes, that was our son, yes, it was. Yes.' We had to *see* that."

I look at him, so large and so gentle. The meager light leaking in from the sink window behind us rinses him in gray. I feel an unbearable motherly tenderness surge through me like gorge rising. "I don't know if Alex wanted to die, exactly," I say. "Maybe just escape. But his anxiety was *so bad*, Rick."

"It wasn't that bad. We found him help. He was getting help, it was helping."

"I think he was hiding bits and pieces of himself from us. He must have been. Why would he have stuffed this little doll full of his memories inside *UnWorld* unless he was planning something? Maybe the branch was shaky, I don't know, in his *mind*. But it seems like he was testing something out. I'm telling you, I think this is a gift. Now, at least, we know something. Now, we have some idea about . . . about what Alex was yearning for."

"Anna, I am begging you. I can't." He is shaking, quivering all over.

I want to ask, *Do you reject* any *explanation of what happened to our son, or just this one?* but I do not. I know the answer. Whatever he has chosen to believe is locked so far inside of him that I don't think he could even tell it to himself.

This is what happens to the sensitive, I suppose, when life lowers its hammer.

Does he have to face it? Maybe he doesn't. Maybe he doesn't need to.

Of course he fucking does. He is the only other person.

"Rick," I say. "I'm asking you to see what Alex did. See our son, Rick. This means he didn't entirely leave us. He wanted some part of himself to remain here. Don't you see?"

He makes an inhuman noise, something like a whinny or a shriek, and then picks up the vase of crocuses on the counter and dashes them, pointlessly, on the floor.

I look at the water, bits of crockery, stray petals, Rick panting like a wounded beast. How disappointing. How stupid. Something heavy comes unpinned in me, swinging loose, and I say all the unconscionable things to him.

Parenting alongside you was exhausting, I say. Whenever you were home, there was this shrill *noise* in my head. For years, I couldn't pinpoint it, then I realized it was the sound *you* made. The sound of your childish need to show everyone in the room, the house, the universe—whoever was there to witness—*no boredom, no loneliness here!* "Master of fucking ceremonies," I snap, unleashed. If he caught Alex staring off into space for twenty seconds, he intervened like a fucking Navy SEAL. He would never leave him, or us, alone.

"My fatal flaw as a parent," Rick sneers. "Believe me, you've made me feel just how despicable my attention is for everyone. I learned pretty well that wasn't something you wanted me to do for you. So I fucking stopped, didn't I?" Then: "Jesus Christ, she *syncs* with you. Let's, just for a moment, assume that I am actually willing to entertain this insane fucking circus you're submerging us in. How could this so-called *explanation* be anything other than an astounding referendum on just how much you are willing to hide from yourself?"

The cruelty is so stunning it pushes both of us into

silence. His lips are still moving, as if he's repeating it back to himself, testing the reverberations. Before he can damage the essential truth of it by trying to say he is sorry, I leave the room.

Later that day, he will throw up. I am not there, but he tells me so, and I believe him.

The aftershocks tremor into a series of softer, more measured conversations over the next ten days.

Me crying silent tears on the couch, facing forward, while Rick muffles his own sobs, his big hands on his face.

Rick's choked wailing reaching me faintly from the downstairs couch, through the floor of Alex's room.

Then a wistful silence between us at opposite ends of the table, like we were the CEO and CFO of a company with no employees left.

On the tenth day after the fight, I pack one small suitcase; it takes me eleven minutes. Rick is teaching, something we agreed upon. I stand in the house for exactly sixty seconds, waiting to pick up a stray scent of valedictory feeling. It is hot, it is Tuesday, and I have to pick up the key to my rented apartment. I leave, turning the handle silently and placing the door in its frame behind me as if someone is asleep.

O n that first night alone, cars sigh past my window for eight hours. I open and close my eyes a hundred times in the seasick dark. When morning arrives, I watch pale light spread across the floorboards like an accident. Then I pour bad coffee into a heavy mug and sit at the long, lean window. The light streams in past the heating pipe, still cold.

The furniture here is nobody's furniture; it hardly knows I'm here. My flip-flops near the door are my only visible belongings. Everything else—five shirts, three pairs of pants, one dress, one hoodie, three bras, nine pairs of underwear— hides itself in one drawer.

For two straight hours, my head feels pleasantly empty, like a drafty church. When the street noises pick up and late morning rolls over, though, I find myself in sudden and dire need of company.

Who?

Jen and Amir don't even seem real to me now. Thinking of them feels like squinting to discern if distant shapes on the shore are rocks or people.

Gradually, I acknowledge the truth. There is only one person left alive I want to talk to.

After only another thirty minutes of hesitating, I pull out my phone and text her.

Cathy is seated at a street-corner café she tells me is around the corner from her own apartment, which, it turns out, is only a ten-minute walk from my own. We spot each other from half a block away, and I stride briskly through the transfiguring curtain of shame that drops down between us. I sit down. My heart feels like a joggling knee.

She regards me with frank amusement and interest, her

mouth corners turned up, no longer an invader in my home.

"I did *not* expect to meet you again," she says. Her voice is warm. "You seemed pretty eager to get me out of the house last time."

"My husband was at work," I say. "He was going to be home soon."

"Ah."

"He teaches," I add. "Ninth-grade English."

"I see."

Our water glasses are filled. I can feel her decide not to ask me any more questions. She is watching me, as if scanning me for something. I wonder if she sees it.

Then she spreads her arms. "Well, like I said when we met, I'm an open book," she says. "Ask me anything you want."

"What was it like?" I ask, after a moment. "You know, receiving the message from her?"

She leans, arms crossed, on the table. "I don't know how to find the language for it. *Physical.* Like someone pressing down on my arm, really hard. The words were so clear in my mind." She shudders a little. "I had thought she was gone. Sam thought I was hallucinating. I was still horribly sick. But it was clear, unmistakable. Almost like a scream."

I think about my own scream, the night in Alex's room when I set her free. "What do you miss most about her. About . . . Aviva?" The name tastes bad in my mouth—odd. Soapy.

She repeats the question, then closes her eyes briefly.

"The *tension*," she says. "Her unlike mind, so close to mine. There was this thrilling asymmetry about her thoughts and impressions, the way they sort of layered atop my own. Everything was more chaotic. I miss the occasional relief from knowing exactly what I thought. But the tension, oh god." She sucks her teeth and stirs her finger at the surface of her water glass, moving the lime wedge and setting bits of pulp drifting.

"I still wake up in the middle of the night sometimes," she says. "I pace my apartment, trying not to walk too loud on the heads of my neighbors. Yearning for that discomfort, that feeling of disagreement. Harboring itself within my body."

She looks off for a minute, then her eyes focus on mine. "I suppose that was *you*."

She stares for a long minute. My cheeks get hot as the silence stretches, but I hold her gaze.

She's right.

It *was* me.

Of course it was.

I notice things about Cathy now: the arch in her eyebrows, the secret dark hair curling out behind her earlobe. I am flooded by a near-sexual desire to talk, to tell her things.

My jaw unhinges. We talk for hours. Two? Three? I tell her about my mother's constant physical exhaustion, her night hours, the injuries—bulging discs, dizzy spells, carpal tunnel—like a planet pulling at us with its gravity. Mom helped old, sick people. She lifted and propped them up and made sure they were comfortable just before they died.

She didn't complain about anything, ever, which is not to say she was happy. I can't recall the sound of her laugh. But she modeled the belief that we were fine all alone so convincingly that I figured holding it up was my end of the bargain.

I was nine years old, her only child, and determined to be the only person in my mother's life who didn't need things from her. I figured out how to do so many things alone—homework, dinner, nighttime routine—but when it came time to fall asleep, I just couldn't manage by myself.

Cathy has pushed her plate away. She leans back in her chair. When the waiter comes to clear the table, neither of us breaks eye contact.

"I don't know why I'm remembering any of this," I say. "Maybe because last night, I had to sleep alone again. But I used to just lie awake, petrified. I'd stare at the dark shapes on the ceiling and just think, *I will never fall asleep.* The only way to calm myself was to call out to my mother, who was lying down in the next room, and I could just *feel* her exhaustion when she said, 'I'm here.' Like it was a life sentence. I was the last person she gave to before she could go to bed, the person who extracted the last bit from her.

"I hated myself for needing her so much. The only way I stopped was by pinching, hard, on my inner thigh. I twisted my skin so hard I would gasp. As the blood flowed to the bruise, I would feel a brief calm. It was a strategy inspired by my own mother, who joked that her migraines took her attention away from her sciatica.

"When I slept through the night without calling to her, I

remember how proud I felt. But also . . . hollow, somehow. I'd finally figured it out. How not to need anything."

I stop. Cathy is still looking at me. Normally, I can't bear uninterrupted eye contact, but this feels distinctly different.

"I don't think I've told anyone that before," I say after a moment, my face growing hot. Then, to change the subject, I say, "So, you've met us both now. What's it like? You know, to meet the upload first, then the person."

She leans forward, close enough that I can see the wrinkles starting to form just below her collarbones, close enough that I can smell her breath. A thin, confidential smile spreads on her face. "Meeting you has been completely its own thing."

R ick opens the door to what used to be our house, his smile wide and tense. He's wearing a blank white T-shirt under a short-sleeved black button-down, and his hair is slightly damp. For this occasion, I'm wearing the only dress I packed, even if I'm not sure what this occasion is.

Cathy is next to me, wearing a loud sleeveless blue-and-yellow print and red cat's-eye glasses I did not know she owned or required. Cathy's presence has been requested. "Oh, and one more thing," Rick said on the phone, sounding tired. It was our first conversation since I moved out. "Sam very much wants Cathy to be a part of this." Before I could react, he added, "I told her it was *okay*, Anna."

Standing side by side, we feel like a declaration. Neither of us are sure of what.

"Hi, guys," Rick says, a humiliating form of address I recognize from his classroom. "Come on in." He steps back with a welcoming arm sweep that squeezes my heart.

Stepping into my own kitchen, after moving out just four weeks ago, I feel mildly concussed. The house looks like it used to when I'd been gone for a few days—clean, mostly, but disheveled and lived-in. I spot several incongruities. An unfamiliar bag slumping on a pulled-out chair, a few older-looking books of Rick's I don't remember—college?—splayed upside down.

In the visible corner of the living room, a bowl of chips sits out on the coffee table next to a liter-sized bottle of raspberry seltzer and two cloudy-looking glasses, one with a single swallow left.

And then Sam looms in front of me like an apparition. She's wearing a long black kimono-style shirt down to her knees over a white tank top, tight black jeans, and combat boots, which squeak as she embraces me—"I'm glad you came," she says into my ear, a sentiment I return, dazed, as my fingers curl around her shoulder blades. I have the odd sensation that this is her house now, and I am the one imposing on her hospitality.

She steps back, makes a self-deprecating joke about her and Rick accidentally dressing alike.

Rick grins at me. I can feel the astonishment, even indignation, on my face in response.

As Sam hugs Cathy—tight, eyes shut, I notice—Rick offers me the same sad-eyed half smile as when he's lost his phone or shattered a plate, an apology without explanation.

After a half second's hesitation, he pulls me close to him. I feel his scruff scratch my temple. The heat of his mood sends me back on my heels a little.

Rick turns to Cathy.

"Hi," he says, a whole sentence.

"Rick," Cathy says back. The freighted manner with which she speaks his name reminds me slightly of Amir's portentousness, and I stifle a disastrous giggle.

"Music?" asks Sam.

Rick nods and smiles, and I marvel again at the new-found comfort of these two.

The music kicks on, way too loud. "Sorry!" Sam calls, also too loudly, as the volume jumps down.

She's chosen something wildly inappropriate to smoothing over an awkward situation—all I hear is a punishing electronic thump, the squealing of machines, a hollering woman. Cathy, of course, recognizes and names the artist immediately, prompting a grudging nod from Rick. Sam joins us at the counter, her boots still making leather noises even as she stands still.

For one very long and unbearable second, we regard one another, adult attendees of a child's tea party, awaiting instructions. There is no topic for us to touch on that doesn't feel explosive. Finally, Sam clears her throat.

"Sorry for always making everything so weird. This feels like the last scene in one of those closed-room mysteries. You know, the part where the detective gets everybody in the room and reveals his findings. I don't have those. Findings, I mean."

She's talking faster than usual. She runs a shaky hand through her hair, takes a breath. Distantly, I wish Jen and Amir were here, then realize Sam hasn't invited them.

"Basically, there was some stuff I needed to say to all of you, and I only have the strength to say it once. I figured it was time for us all to be in one place, anyway. Rick, Anna . . . I know I should've been at the funeral. I'm sorry I didn't come. I really, *really* wanted to be there. But I was getting dressed in my house and . . ." She falters. I reach for her, but she swats my hand, then mumbles, *sorry*.

"My excuse doesn't even make sense," she goes on. "Nobody at school really even knew that Alex and I were *friends*. Most kids in my grade probably barely wondered why I stopped coming to school. But I just felt like—if I was there, everybody would know I was responsible. So I stayed home."

She looks directly at Rick. "I wanted to say—I know that it was weird that we were friends. Thank you for always allowing me to come over. Thank you for allowing me to be around your son." His face is gray, but he holds her gaze.

Then she turns to me. "Anna, when that woman across the street, Vicki whatshername, came out onto her porch that one time just to yell at me and Alex, to tell me it was 'unnatural' for me to hang out with 'young boys,' you defended me. You told her to mind her business. I didn't say anything then, because it was too awkward. But—thanks. I appreciated that."

At my side, Cathy is gripping my hand, hard. Tears are pouring down Sam's face, but otherwise she is Sam—lucid, eerily calm, composed. Her voice, as she says all of this, is conversational.

"Anyway, when I was getting dressed for the funeral, all I could think of was that woman," she says. "Vicki whatsher-name, screaming in my face. Like someone there would point at me, and—" She shook her head.

"Honestly, I was pretty sure it *was* my fault. Like, maybe I'd manifested this shitty reality with my movie and cor-rupted him, somehow. Like, maybe if I'd never known him, he'd still be alive." Rick and I both start to object, but she silences us. "Please," she says harshly. "I just need to get through this.

"I think that's why I first started obsessing about his rela-tionship with your upload, Anna," she says. "Maybe that was a way for it not to be my fault. When I burst in crying on your dinner with my parents that night, I was coming to tell you all about it, but then I heard it in my head. 'Guess what, Anna, I've been so worried that your son's death was all my fault. Turns out . . .'" She makes a face. "When I realized what I was about to do, I just left."

She turns to Cathy. "I know you feel out of place here. But you're not. She—Aviva—chose you for a reason." Her voice hitches for the first time on Aviva's name, and she swallows hard. "And, uh, I don't know if either of you can still talk to her"—Cathy stifles a small cry, puts a hand to her mouth, and shakes her head hard, once—"well, I just wanted to tell her. I don't think it's *her* fault, either.

"The part I can't figure out is *when* Alex decided. Did he plan it the whole way up? I just can't make myself believe that. He was so goofy, so normal. Did he maybe just go up to the edge and have this *one* thought?

"We used to always talk about how a stray thought could be dangerous. What would happen if you had this idea, and suddenly you just acted on it? I have this dream where it happens. I say 'Hey' as he walks away. That's all I get out of my mouth. Just 'hey.' But he turns around and starts to move like he's coming back. Then the dream ends.

"I think that's all I needed to do. He could have been stopped. I think all I would have needed to do is say something to him, to get him to walk back to me. I was sitting right there, and he could have been stopped."

She stops. "I'm sorry," she says. And then she starts sobbing. She buries her face in Rick's shoulder.

I hug Sam afterward, murmuring that we love her, that she was like a sister to Alex, that she will always be family. But I recognized the fatherly way Rick clung to her. She won't be needing me.

A part of me envies her, just a little.

Cathy moves toward Rick. He shrinks as if she has moved to stick her tongue in his mouth. Instead, she rests a stiff-armed hand on his shoulder and murmurs something noncommittal, gratitude for being allowed to join in as witness. He nods at her, uncomfortably, and Cathy and Sam exchange meaningful looks. The two of them wander into the living room, and Rick and I are alone. His eyes are reddened, like weeping sores.

"So," I manage. "You and Sam seem to be spending more time together."

He grins. "One night, a couple weeks ago, she just showed up and asked if I wanted to watch a movie with her."

"What movie?"

"The one where the teenagers disembowel each other," he says. "Alex loved it." After that, she'd suggested others—an Italian horror movie where the portal to hell opens up beneath a house and a Polish movie where a village kills a woman and then one by one succumbs to a horrible wasting illness.

"Cheery," I say. "How were they?"

He shrugs. "Expressionist. Lots of odd angles, cool shadows. She's pretty sharp." He finds my eyes. "She comes over almost every night now." The unspoken invitation hangs in the air, and I read the rest in his gaze: *I'd still be your protector, too, if you'd only show me how.*

"Rick—" I don't know how to ask. I feel him hesitating toward me. "Could I have a moment alone? In Alex's room?"

He stops, looking stung. Then he smiles sadly, nods, and leaves.

I wait until his trail of hurt and confusion clears.

I walk up the steps, push open the door, and think, *Now it's just the three of us.*

Alex, you were always afraid of getting lost. You worried you'd wind up someplace so far away nobody would find you.

The world seems so hard, so solid and unyielding, when you look at it. I've had to close my eyes to learn something else is true: The world is constantly dissolving, constantly reassembling itself. I sense points of egress everywhere, Alex, and yet when I reach out my hand, there is no give. Nothing. The world blocks you in, closes itself to your touch. Pick up a vase and let go, and you learn again: no admittance. The farther it drops the more certain you become.

But yet again—*how* hard, *how* certain? Isn't the hard ground itself pockmarked with tunnels and burrows, and farther down, isn't it all just a jigsaw puzzle, surfing atop hot liquid? Down there, where the skull plates shift farther apart, the molten brain tissue pours forth, hardening the second it touches coolness. How wide does one of those cracks have to yawn open for something, for someone, to skitter inside?

Did you see, or imagine, a crack, Alex? Did you think there would be a hand to catch you?

I need to find you.

How much of you wanted oblivion? I'll never know.

What I know is that you left a little bit of yourself behind. You hid yourself, or as much as you could squirrel away, and you waited. You wandered forth and came out to greet your discoverer. You came out to greet . . . who? Her?

No. Me. You waited for *me*. You saw what she was. The freest part of me. You so clearly saw how all the parts of me you couldn't talk to were there for you, in her. That was the part of me that left when she did. Now, the two of you are together, somewhere.

What enters you always leaves its traces. I've felt you. Something different than normal, lately—flashes. An expectancy in the air. Someone or something. I don't mention it to anyone. Just yesterday, I had it the strongest, lying in bed: someone, something, waiting with all of their might, to speak. A mouth, sealed, working to tear itself open. I didn't move for half an hour. I held open my eyes until I blinked tears. Two hours, then realized—no. Not today.

The two of you found each other, and when you did, you left me behind. But I am still here—an old house, for sure, but not quite abandoned. The world is widening open, and I know that one day the thing will happen that nobody else knows. You will enter into me. I will receive you. I will be graced by it. I will find my way to you, through the hole you created. That's what wounding does. It creates a hole.

Somewhere in that slipstream, the two of you are intermingled, whispering.

I'm waiting.

Come back to me.

Acknowledgments

The last time I attempted fiction, I was thirteen. Roughly eighty pages into a David Eddings–indebted fantasy yarn for my seventh-grade English teacher, Mrs. Nugent, I lost the thread. Whatever quality is required to commit made-up stories to the page—nerve, will, self-belief—vacated me and didn't return for another twenty-three years, when I wrote the first twelve pages for what would, eventually, become *UnWorld*.

Finding the guts to make this leap at age thirty-six came with its fair share of second-guessing. I often felt like a tricycle-riding bear or, worse, a middle-aged man attempting his first novel. I'm forever grateful to the friends with whom I shared my earliest attempts: Hannah Carlen, Corban Goble, Jeremy Gordon, Elizabeth Gold, Alex Naidus, Dave Tompkins.

Thanks to my agent, Anna Sproul-Latimer, who's invested more time in my eight-year journey from music journalist to memoirist to novelist than might be expected of any sane

Acknowledgments

person. Thank you for poring over countless early versions of this book; for subjecting my fictional characters to prolonged therapy sessions in our text and phone conversations. I am forever grateful you're in my corner.

My vision for *UnWorld* was born when Jordan Pavlin edited *Once More We Saw Stars;* I knew when we met that, one day, I wanted to work on a novel with her. Jordan, bringing these pages to you, and feeling you lavish your attention upon them, was the definition of my dreams coming true. Without your fierce belief, this novel would have never existed.

I'm grateful to Tracy O'Neill, whose 2018 Catapult class workshopped those first twelve pages. You spotted the potential in my material even then, and graciously told me that I needed to keep going.

I enrolled in an MFA program to find my way through *UnWorld,* and each of my Bennington advisers helped me locate a puzzle piece. Deirdre McNamer loved my characters even at their most larval. David Gates crossed out almost everything I wrote, allowing me to fill that space with better writing. Stuart Nadler coaxed me into writing scenes that breathed. Deep into the pandemic, Derek Palacio helped me see the shape of the eventual novel on Zoom calls from the back seat of my Volkswagen.

Although the on-campus residencies were cut short by the pandemic, I remain grateful for the memories I made. Special thanks to Caro Claire Burke, Sarah Andrews Chamberlin, Max Torrens Frazier, Puloma Ghosh, Davin Malasarn, Rena J. Mosteirin, Carmen Radley, Jeannie Riess, Cristina Olivetti Spencer, Mary Alice Stewart, and Natalie Warther.

Thank you for the invaluable feedback from my writers' group of 2018 and 2019 (which I still miss!): Suleika Jaouad, Tara Westover, Melissa Febos, Jordan Kisner, Scott Frank, and Jon Batiste. Extra thanks, as always, to Suleika, for providing the beacon we rallied around and for leading a life by spiritual example.

For intellectual stimulation, friendship, and constant friendly queries about "how the novel's going": Cat Zhang, Jenn Pelly, Anna Brown Massey, Adam Tenninbaum and Taryn Gould, J. Edward Keyes, Heather Traher and Bryon Kent, Martina Prinzis, Jessica Rich.

Thank you to neighbors Pat and Natia for letting me use their adjoining apartment as my personal writing studio whenever they were gone; to Heath Fradkoff for letting me camp out in his abandoned work space during the zombie-apocalypse days of the shutdown.

To Alua Arthur, whose bright soul, enormous smile, and boundless enthusiasm brought me inspiration and joy during a tough time in 2023.

Thank you to Charlotte Elkin, whose work in Internal Family Systems therapy both helped inform this book and altered the course of my life.

Thanks to my parents, Joni and Arthur Greene, for encouraging and safeguarding their dreamy and distracted kid; thanks to my brother, John Serdinsky, the first writer I ever admired, who read that seventh-grade fantasy opus and critiqued it as seriously as any workshop submission.

Thank you, now and forever, to Grandma Suz, for always being Harrison's safe harbor.

Acknowledgments

Thanks to Bruce and Monica, for building our perfect house and for bringing us into your upstate community.

I'm grateful to our nervous but steadfast goldendoodle, Obie, whose chaotic puppyhood set this book's completion back six months, bare minimum, but who rested his head faithfully on my feet during many solo writer's retreats away from the rest of the family.

Thank you to my son, Harrison, who has watched me leave for entire weekends with understanding in his eyes because "Daddy needs to write." Harrison, I will forever worship your boundless creativity and imagination, as well as your moral clarity and deep kindness. You are my favorite person in the entire universe, buddy. Watching you make your way in life is like watching a tree grow overhead; you're only eight, but I already feel myself looking up to you.

And thank you, finally, to Stacy, to whom I owe more than it is possible at this point to even say.

Thank you for stepping in countless times to give me space to write. For extending a limitless trust and belief I was never sure I merited as I chased whatever it was I saw in my head. For encouraging me to visualize my career pivot as the turning of "a Mack truck or an ocean liner." For listening to me talk about my half-formed ideas for *UnWorld* for enough hours to fill several uninterrupted days. For pushing this book uphill with your inspiration and feedback the countless times I was rudderless and discouraged.

Thank you for charting a seeker's path through a world that grows ever more violent, fearful, and uncertain, and for continuing to be my partner and my companion. We've done this before. We'll keep doing it for as long as life allows and I'm sure we'll continue later, on some other plane.

You're still the only person I trust with my heart, and I would be in darkness without you next to me.

Thank you, Stacy.

A NOTE ABOUT THE AUTHOR

Jayson Greene is the author of *Once More We Saw Stars* and a contributing writer and former senior editor at *Pitchfork*. He lives in Brooklyn with his wife and son. This is his first novel.

A NOTE ON THE TYPE

This book was set in Adobe Garamond. Designed for the Adobe Corporation by Robert Slimbach, the fonts are based on types first cut by Claude Garamond (ca. 1480–1561). It is to Garamond that we owe the letter we now know as "old style." He gave to his letters an elegance and feeling of movement that won him an immediate reputation and the patronage of Francis I of France.

Typeset by Scribe
Philadelphia, Pennsylvania

Book design by Pei Loi Koay